THIS BOOK BELONGS TO

\- - - - - - - - - - - - - - - - -

\- - - - - - - - - - - - - -

Books by Duncan Ball

Emily Eyefinger
Emily Eyefinger, Secret Agent
Emily Eyefinger and the Lost Treasure
Emily Eyefinger and the Black Volcano
Emily Eyefinger's Alien Adventure
Emily Eyefinger and the Devil Bones

My Dog's a Scaredy-cat
(illustrated by Craig Smith)

Piggott Place
Piggotts in Peril

Selby's Secret
Selby Speaks
Selby Screams
Selby Supersnoop
Selby Spacedog
Selby Snowbound
Selby Surfs
Selby Snaps!
Selby Splits
Selby's Stardom
Selby's Joke Book
Selby's Side-Splitting Joke Book
Selby's Selection

SELBY SPLITS

DUNCAN BALL

illustrated by Allan Stomann

Angus&Robertson
An imprint of HarperCollins*Publishers*

Acknowledgements: First and foremost, the author would like to thank Allan Stomann for many years of illustrating the Selby books. And, once again, many thanks to Rod Morrison for his prizewinning editing; Barbara Mobbs for her assiduous agenting, and all those at HarperCollins*Publishers* who have helped to breathe life into the old dog: Barrie Hitchon, Shona Martyn, Lisa Berryman, Cristina Rodrigues, Laura Tricker, Natasha Duivenbode, Louisa Dear and the rest. And to all of Selby's and my email pals. Among them, Jenna, who wanted to know why the Selby books were in the fiction section of the library, and Ms X (whose name I've sworn never to reveal) who 'actually fell in love' with Selby.

Angus&Robertson
An imprint of HarperCollins*Publishers*, Australia

First published in Australia in 2001
Reprinted in 2001, 2002 (twice)
by HarperCollins*Publishers* Pty Limited
ABN 36 009 913 517
A member of the HarperCollins*Publishers* (Australia) Pty Limited Group
www.harpercollins.com.au

HarperCollins*Publishers*
25 Ryde Road, Pymble, Sydney, NSW 2073, Australia
31 View Road, Glenfield, Auckland 10, New Zealand
77–85 Fulham Palace Road, London W6 8JB, United Kingdom
Hazelton Lanes, 55 Avenue Road, Suite 2900, Toronto, Ontario M5R 3L2
and 1995 Markham Road, Scarborough, Ontario M1B 5M8, Canada
10 East 53rd Street, New York NY 10022, USA

National Library of Australia Cataloguing-in-Publication data:

Ball, Duncan, 1941– .
Selby splits.
ISBN 0 207 19780 6.
1. Dogs – Juvenile fiction. I. Stomann, Allan. II. Title.
A823.3

Printed and bound in Australia by Griffin Press on 80gsm Econoprint

9 8 7 6 5 4 02 03 04 05

For Jasper, the cat

(Just in case you're secretly reading this book)

Author's Note

I don't know where Selby lives. I only know that he lives in a town that he calls 'Bogusville'. I don't even know his real name. But I've talked to him for many hours on the telephone and I've met him a few times when he's turned up at schools I've been visiting. At these times he always wears his dog suit so no one will recognise him if they see him later without it.

Over the years I've got to know Selby very well so I was especially surprised at something he said while he was telling me about his latest adventures. It was late at night and we'd been talking on the phone for hours. At first I wasn't sure I'd heard him correctly.

'Did you say that Willy and Billy fell in love with you?' I asked.

'Yes,' he said, 'and then there was the time I was trapped in this tomb and there were all these skeletons around and —'

'In love? Willy and Billy?' I said. 'You hate Willy and Billy and they hate you.'

'Hate is a very strong word,' he said.

'But you do,' I said. 'You hate them. You've told me yourself.'

'Okay, I hate them but they fell in love with me anyway,' he said. 'It was very embarrassing. Don't you want to hear about how I was attacked by a huge spider or about how I helped the New York cops or how I inherited a mansion or how I split in two?'

'First tell me about Willy and Billy falling in love with you.'

'Aunt Jetty fell in love with me too.'

'Aunt Jetty? Willy and Billy's mother? She's as bad as they are! Forget the other stories and tell me about this now!'

'Okay, it was like this . . .'

Well I won't spoil it for you. Have a look at the story called 'Madame Mascara's Passion Potion' if you want to be amazed (and embarrassed) too.

Duncan Ball

Contents

Reflecting	xi
Selby Spiderdog	1
Dear Deirdre	15
O Bum, O Bum	29
Cloud Blaster	32
The Tomb of the Dancing Dead	43
Selby's (Great) Expectations	60
The Worm	77
Neat Streets	78
Selby's New York Adventure	91
Sticks and Stones	105
Madame Mascara's Passion Potion	119
My Itch Attack	136
Selby Survives	137
Santa Selby	150
O Handsome Me	164
Selby Splits	166
Through the Licking-glass	192

REFLECTING

The word **reflecting** can mean thinking. Right now I'm **reflecting** on what mirrors do. Since mirrors reflect, I guess I'm **reflecting** about **reflecting**! Have you ever wondered who it is that looks out of the mirror when you look in? Is it you? Or is it somebody else who only looks like you but isn't? Mirrors are weird!

I'm not going to say anything else right now and I'm not going to tell you how I split. You'll have to see for yourself. I just hope you like these exciting stories about me — the only talking dog in Australia and, perhaps, the world.

Happy reading!

Selby

SELBY SPIDERDOG

'This spider doesn't rock,' Postie Paterson said, holding up the glass case with the huge spider in it. 'That's why the spider expert is coming to have a look at her.'

'Is she supposed to rock?' Mrs Trifle asked.

'Yes. Amy is an Amazon Rocking Spider. Rocking spiders rock. They rock back and forth before they pounce. Amy just sits there and twitches. She hasn't rocked since we got her. Do you want a closer look?' Postie said, opening the case and grabbing Amy by the back. 'She's the most valuable animal we have in the zoo.'

'Please keep her away from me!' Mrs Trifle said. 'I have that a-rack-nose thing.'

'Is there something wrong with your nose? Oh, I get it — you've got *arachnophobia*. You're afraid of spiders.'

'Petrified,' said Mrs Trifle. 'Especially of big black hairy ones with tufts of orange fur sticking out all over the place and beady black eyes that stare at you.'

'In other words, like Amy here,' Postie said. 'Don't worry, Amy's harmless. She might have a go at small animals with those fangs of hers but nothing as big as a human.'

'Just keep the bolt on the top of that case closed,' Mrs Trifle said. 'Now you'd better get on with your letter deliveries. I'll pick up this spider expert from the airport. What's the woman's name again?'

'How could you forget — it's Dr Webb. Dr Charlotte Webb.'

'See you back here later,' Mrs Trifle said. 'Just put Amy in the study.'

'Sheeeeeeesh!' Selby thought after Postie and Mrs Trifle had gone. 'I hate spiders too! I don't even like little ones and this one's *ginormous*!'

Selby opened the door to the study and peered in at Amy.

'Postie put the case right behind the chair,' he thought. 'I'll have to move it to pull the chair out and get to the computer. I haven't answered any emails for yonks but now's the perfect time because the Trifles are both out.'

Selby crouched down.

'Those tiny eyes — sheeeeesh! — they're staring straight at me! They're burning holes in me. Stop looking at me.'

Selby put his paw out to push the case back. Amy gave a twitch. The moment Selby's paw touched the case, she leapt at it, hitting the glass and bouncing back.

'Yikes!' Selby gasped. 'She went for me! But what am I scared of?🐾 she's in there and I'm out here.'

Selby reached out and slid the case along the floor. Once again, Amy had a go at him through the glass. But this time Selby kept pushing.

'*Nya nya.* Serves you right if you hurt yourself,' Selby sang.

Selby jumped up onto the chair, swivelled around and turned on the computer.

🐾 *Paw note: This is my own invention — a question comma! You can use it in the middle of a sentence. Look for question commas and exclamation commas in this book.* S

'Now to check my emails. Let's see what the kiddies have to say.'

What Selby didn't notice when he swivelled the chair around was that part of the back of the chair had caught the bolt at the top of Amy's case. That would have been okay except it slid the bolt sideways, unlocking the top of the case.

Inside, Amy gave a shudder and then a twitch. Then a furry black leg quietly pushed up the top of the case. This leg was followed by another and another. Soon four of Amy's eight legs were hooked over the edge of the case. Her beady eyes stared up at the back of Selby's chair.

As Selby read his first email, he had no idea that a large hairy creature was creeping its way up the back of his chair.

'Oh, I love getting emails from kids,' Selby thought. 'It makes me feel soooooooooo famous. Let's see what this one says.'

DEAR SELBY,

I LOVE YOUR BOOKS AND I LOVE YOU TOO. YOU ARE MY VERY FAVOURITE DOG IN THE WHOLE WORLD. COULD YOU PLEASE PLEASE PLEASE — PRETTY PLEASE WITH SUGAR ON TOP — TELL ME YOUR REAL NAME AND

WHERE YOU REALLY LIVE? (I PROMISE I WON'T TELL ANYONE!!!!!!!!!!!!)
FROM YOUR NUMBER ONE FAN,
AMY

Selby had a little chuckle over the girl's name and then started typing an email back.

HIYA AMY,
THANX FOR YOUR EMAIL. I'D LOVE TO TELL YOU MY REAL NAME BUT I CAN'T. SOME DAY YOU MIGHT TALK IN YOUR SLEEP AND SOMEBODY MIGHT HEAR YOU AND THEN THEY'D KNOW MY NAME AND THEY'D FIND ME AND MY PEACEFUL LIFE WOULD BE RUINED FOREVER.

By now Amy was on the back of Selby's chair, reaching out with one leg towards his back. Selby kept typing very slowly with one claw at a time.

AND, HEY, GUESS WHAT? YOU WOULDN'T BELIEVE THIS BUT THERE'S ANOTHER AMY HERE. ONLY THIS AMY IS A BIG HAIRY —

Suddenly one of Amy's legs touched Selby's back.

'What's that?' he thought. 'It feels like something is crawling on me. No, that's silly. I've got myself so scared of spiders that now I'm feeling things. Let's see about this email now . . . Hmmm, no, that definitely does feel like something on my back. Don't panic. Just turn around slowly and have a —'

'Yeeeooouuuwww!' Selby screamed.

Selby jumped forward onto the desk, throwing Amy onto the floor.

'Get back in your box!' he yelled. 'I've got to get out of here!'

Selby was about to make a dash for the door when Amy leapt up in the air.

'She was going to grab me!' Selby squealed. 'The little devil is stalking me!'

Selby jumped in the other direction: over the computer and onto the windowsill.

'I'll get out through the window,' he thought, 'then I'll run around the house and close the study door and she'll be trapped in here.'

While Selby struggled with the window he glanced over his shoulder. There, on the floor, was the dark shape of the spider coming towards him.

'The window's stuck!' Selby cried. 'I can't get it open!'

Amy twitched and then leapt straight towards Selby. Selby, seeing the huge hairy spider hurtling towards him, leapt even higher, grabbing the light globe that dangled from the ceiling.

'This is crazy,' Selby thought. 'She's got *me* acting like a spider!'

Selby swung forward, falling to the ground. Then, in a single bound he was out the door and holding it firmly closed.

'Okay, she's trapped now,' he thought. 'I'm sure the spiderwoman will be able to get her back in her case. No one will ever know that it was my fault that the case got unlocked. They'll just think that Amy twitched a lot and the bolt slid open or something.'

Selby heaved a sigh of relief.

'Oops, the computer's still on. They'll know that it was me who turned it on. Who else could have done it? They'll know I'm not just an ordinary non-talking, non-computer-turning-on-ing dog. But, hang on, Amy could have jumped on the keyboard and turned it on.'

Selby was just heaving a second sigh when something else occurred to him.

'My secret email account is on the screen! The Trifles might work out that I'm a talking, typing, emailing dog who uses the secret name "Selby"! I've got to turn the computer off.'

As Selby's mind raced, a thick black leg made its way under the bottom of the door. This leg was followed by another and another. Then, hearing the quiet scraping sound that huge black spiders with tufts of orange hair make when they squeeze under doors, Selby looked down to see Amy.

'Yowza!' Selby screamed as Amy chased him through the dining room and into the kitchen.

Selby grabbed the only thing he could reach — a plastic mixing bowl — and threw it over Amy.

'Gotcha!' Selby said. 'Now all I need is something to slide under the bowl so I can carry you back to your case.'

Selby was searching through a cupboard when he noticed the bowl making its way across the floor.

'Hey! Come back here!' Selby cried.

Selby leapt on the bowl only to have it start moving again, this time with him riding on top.

'I'm surfing a spider! Save me! Stop!' he cried.

The bowl went faster and faster until it hit the corner of a carpet, turning over and throwing Selby on his back on the floor. Selby looked up to see Amy sitting on his chest.

'Get off me!' he screamed, shaking her off and grabbing a broom.

Selby held the broom out to keep Amy away. Instead she slowly climbed onto the end of it.

'Good one,' Selby thought. 'I'll just carry her to the study.'

In the study, Selby put the end of the broom with Amy on it into the case.

'Okay you can let go now,' he said, giving the broom a little shake.

But instead of letting go, Amy suddenly ran up the broom handle towards Selby's paws. Without thinking, Selby gave the broom an almighty swing, flinging Amy back into the dining room where she scurried away.

'Come back here!' Selby yelled. 'Okay, no more Mr-Nice-picking-you-gently-up-with-the-broom-Dog. It's whammo blammo smasho time. I don't care if you're worth a million dollars, I'm going to get you back in that case even if you're unconscious. Here, spidey spidey.'

Selby searched everywhere for the spider but she was nowhere to be found.

'Mrs Trifle and the spiderwoman will be back soon. I'd better at least turn off the computer. Hang on, maybe I can find out something about Amazon Rocking Spiders from a website that'll help me catch Amy. A spider with a *web*site,' he thought, chuckling to himself. 'That's a good one.'

Sure enough, within seconds, Selby was reading the Amazon Rocking Spider web page.

'. . . very rare . . . hunts by day . . . loves insects and other small animals . . . won't attack humans . . . very territorial . . . Nothing here,' Selby said to himself as he turned off the computer. 'Very *territorial*? They don't like other animals in *their* territory. That's it!'

Selby climbed into Amy's case and pulled the lid closed. Soon a hairy leg — and then seven more hairy legs — came into the study.

'I'm in your case,' he sang out. 'And I'm not coming out.'

In a minute, Amy was there, looking at him through the glass just millimetres from his nose.

'It worked. Now to do the old switcheroo.'

Selby slowly lifted the lid of the case and stepped out.

'So you won't have a go at a human, Amy?' he said.

With this Selby stood up on his hind legs and stretched himself up as high as he could. Amy flattened herself to the ground.

'Oh, so now you're afraid of me,' Selby said in his deepest voice. 'Okay, back you go.'

Selby reached down and grabbed Amy just the way he'd seen Postie pick her up.

'Why didn't I think of that before?' he wondered as he closed the study door, just as Mrs Trifle and Dr Webb came home. 'Ouch, Amy scratched me!'

'She's in here,' Mrs Trifle said, leading the spider expert into the study.

'Just as I thought,' the woman said. 'After Mr Paterson told me about her on the phone, I realised why she wasn't rocking. She's not sick, she's just not an Amazon Rocking Spider.'

'Isn't she?'

'No, she's a close relative, though: an Amazon *Twitching* Spider, the deadliest spider on earth.'

'Goodness me!' Mrs Trifle exclaimed. 'And Postie *touched* her.'

'He's lucky to be alive then. One tiny scratch from this little beastie and things begin to happen.'

'Gulp,' Selby thought. 'What sorts of things?'

'What sorts of things?' Mrs Trifle asked.

'First there's the tingling —'

'Tingling?' Selby thought. 'But I'm tingling all over!'

'Then there's a numbness that creeps up the legs —'

'I can feel it!' Selby screamed silently. 'It's creeping up my legs!'

'After that the throat seizes up and you gasp for breath —'

'What a coincidence,' Mrs Trifle said, 'Selby is gasping for breath right now. Then what happens?'

'You sweat. Your body freezes, then death follows,' the woman said.

'Selby is dripping with sweat,' Mrs Trifle said. 'If I didn't know better I'd have thought he'd been bitten by that spider. What a riot.'

'Riot schmiot!' Selby thought. 'I'm frozen. I'm dying and it's all my fault! And all because I wanted to answer my emails. Now I've got to talk to Mrs Trifle. In the few minutes I have left on this earth, I want to thank her and Dr Trifle for everything they've done for me. I've decided — I'm going to talk.'

Selby looked up at Mrs Trifle and Dr Webb. He was about to say, 'Sorry to shock you like this, but I have to tell you that I know how to talk — and read and write. But I just made a silly mistake and Amy bit me, so I guess it's hello and goodbye,' when Mrs Trifle got in first and said:

'How long does it take for a spider like Amy to kill someone?'

'Five seconds,' the spiderwoman said. 'Six seconds, tops. Nobody's ever made it past seven.'

'Five, six, seven seconds?' Selby thought as his breathing returned to normal. 'It's already been at least a minute. I haven't been bitten! I'm going to live!'

'Poor old thing,' Mrs Trifle said, stroking Selby. 'I think he was having a bad dream.'

'You're not wrong,' Selby thought. 'This spider business has been a real nightmare.'

DEAR DEIRDRE

'I just love to read the "Dear Deirdre" column,' Selby thought as he secretly read the back page of the *Bogusville Banner*. 'Deirdre is so good the way she answers questions about people's problems. She really understands.'

That day there was a letter from a man who lived with his old mother. His girlfriend wanted to marry him but didn't want to live with his mother. At the end of the letter, instcad of signing his name, he wrote 'Don't Know What To Do'.

Deirdre answered:

> Dear Don't Know What To Do,
> Is it possible for you and your future wife to live near your mother? If so,

> tell your mother that you will continue to look after her but that you must be with the woman you love. Talk to her. She will understand that, like a young bird in a nest, there comes a time when we have to spread our wings and fly.
> Deirdre

'Spread our wings and fly,' Selby thought. 'Deirdre is so wonderful. She's so sensitive. I just love her!'

'Hey, you filthy dog! Get off that newspaper!'

Selby raised his head to see the huge shape of Aunt Jetty 🐾 towering above him. But before he could move, she'd whipped the *Bogusville Banner* out from under him.

'Jetty,' Mrs Trifle said to her sister. 'Be nice to Selby.'

'I'm sorry, but the Slaghaven Slugs thrashed

🐾 *Paw note: I hate Aunt Jetty and she hates me. If you hate her too then read the story 'Selby Slugs Aunt Jetty' in the book* Selby Snowbound. *It's sooooooo cool!*
S

the Poshfield Poteroos yesterday,' Aunt Jetty explained. 'I want to see what Jock Bashem has to say about it.'

Aunt Jetty read Jock Bashem's 'Time Out' column to herself and giggled as she read.

'Hey, listen to this,' she said to her sister. '"The Poteroos were dead meat for a savage Slugs side. From the minute Crasher Asher bounced off the bench screaming for Poteroo blood, the Pots knew they'd end up with their brains in their boots. At the end of the fifteen-nil slaughter there was nothing left of the losers but arms and legs strewn around the field." Isn't that great!'

'Goodness,' Mrs Trifle said. 'Were there just arms and legs lying around?'

'No, of course not. But don't you love the way Jock writes? It's — it's poetry!'

'I've never been much for sport,' Mrs Trifle said.

'Well I adore him,' Aunt Jetty squealed. 'There's a real man — my kind of man. I'm going to race right home and email him. I'll tell him how much I love his column.'

'Poet schmoet,' Selby thought. 'He's about as sensitive as a meat cleaver.'

Selby waited another week for another *Bogusville Banner* to read 'Dear Deirdre' again. This time there was a letter from a girl.

> Dear Deirdre,
> I am a teenage girl and I have a little sister. When I'm out of the house, she like puts on my make-up and that. I'm like, 'Don't do that!' And she's like, 'You can't stop me!' And I'm like, 'If you ever touch my lipstick, slugface, I'll kill you!' And she's like, 'Go ahead, I dare you.' I want to kill her but my parents might get mad and that.
> Distressed

'Hmmm,' Selby hmmmed. 'Now there's a real problem. I wonder how Dear Deirdre will handle it. Let's see now . . .'

> Dear Distressed,
> Don't kill your sister. First of all it could be messy. And you might miss her one day. Stay calm and sit down with her and explain that cosmetics are very expensive. Tell her that you'll give her some of

> her own on her next birthday but to please respect your personal property. I'm sure she'll understand. If she doesn't then buy a strong metal box, put your cosmetics in it and padlock it shut till your sister is older.
> Deirdre

'She's sooooooo good,' Selby thought. 'She's funny but she's also wise. I wonder what Deirdre looks like. I'm dying of curiosity. I reckon she's tall and slim with long blonde hair. I'll bet she's gorgeous. Hey, I know, maybe I'll just pop down to the *Bogusville Banner* and find out for myself.'

Minutes later Selby was at the newspaper office, standing on his hind legs and peering through the front window.

'How will I know which one she is?' he wondered. 'Oh, this is easy, there's only one woman in the place. She's not very tall — she's quite short in fact. And she's a bit plump. And she doesn't have long blonde hair but short dark hair. People never look the way you expect. Okay, so she's also not gorgeous but, to me, she's the most beautiful person on earth.'

Selby crept through the open door for a closer look at Deirdre. But, as he did, a man, chewing a huge cigar, spun around in his chair.

'Beat it, dog!' he yelled. 'Get your tail out of here before I kick you through the window!'

Selby ran for the door but the man had already rolled up a copy of the newspaper and smacked him with it. In a second, Selby was out the door and rubbing his ear with his paw.

'I'll tell you what,' Selby thought. 'That Jock Bashem is *exactly* what I expected! What a mongrel! No wonder Aunt Jetty likes him — he looks like her!'

Selby hung around outside the office as night fell. Finally the office closed and the reporters came out. Some of them went into the restaurant next door, The Spicy Onion. But Deirdre said that she had to cook dinner for her mother and walked off down the street with Selby following close behind.

'I'd love to just go up and talk to her,' he thought, 'but I don't dare. I'd frighten her to death. I love everything about her — the way she walks, the way she runs her fingers through her hair. I've got to know more about her.'

Selby followed Deirdre to her house and

peered through the window. Inside she kissed an old woman on the forehead and then set about making the evening meal.

‘No wonder she understood so much about “Don’t Know What To Do’s” problem,’ Selby thought. ‘She looks after her mum too. I’ll bet she doesn’t have a boyfriend. Oh how I wish I could be her boyfriend.’

After a while the old woman went to bed and Deirdre sat watching TV. Selby went home that night and lay on his mat unable to sleep because of thoughts of Deirdre.

‘I love her,’ he said to himself. ‘But she can never love me because I’m a dog. I mean the Trifles love me but that’s different. Oh, woe, this is almost the worst problem anyone ever had! There’s no answer to it! I’ll just have to try to forget her. I wish I’d never started reading “Dear Dcirdrc”. Now hang on! That could be the answer! Maybe *she* can solve my problem!’

Selby dashed to the Trifles’ computer and wrote an email:

> Dear Deirdre,
> I have a big problem. You see I’m in love with a woman but I don’t know how to tell her.
> Hopelessly in Love

Selby had to wait a week for Deirdre's answer:

> Dear Hopelessly,
> You must follow your heart. Find the right moment and tell her how you feel about her. Do not keep the object of your affection in the dark. She has to know. If she cannot love you, that is a different matter but you cannot let your love go unspoken or it will eat away at your heart like acid eats through steel.
> Deirdre

'Like acid eats through steel,' Selby read aloud. 'Now *that's* poetry. But hang on, what if she knew that I'm a dog? — a talking dog, but still a dog. I wonder if she'd say that I should go up to her and tell her that I love her. I should have said that in my email. But if I came right out with it she'd have thought I was a nutcase and wouldn't have published my email. I'll write to her again.'

> DEAR DEIRDRE,
> I FORGOT TO TELL YOU THAT THERE'S A BIG BIG BIG PROBLEM ABOUT TELLING THIS WOMAN THAT I

LOVE HER. IT'S A SECRET OF MINE THAT MIGHT
KNOCK HER SOCKS OFF.
HOPELESSLY IN LOVE

Once again Selby waited to read 'Dear Deirdre' but this time, just as the *Bogusville Banner* was delivered, Aunt Jetty dashed in the door and snatched it so that she could read Jock Bashem's column.

'What a man!' she said to her sister when she'd finished. 'Not like that pathetic woman who writes "Dear Deirdre". Do you read that column?'

'No, I'm afraid I don't,' Mrs Trifle said.

'Listen to this,' Aunt Jetty said. 'There's this bloke who calls himself Hopelessly in Love. He hasn't even got the guts to tell this woman that he loves her. What a wimp! Listen to what Deirdre says:'

Dear Hopelessly,
Okay so there's something about yourself that might shock her. But you must tell her anyway. We all have our secrets. Don't torture yourself any longer. Grab her and press her to you. Plant a big juicy kiss on her lips and she will

> melt in your arms. Say, 'Darling, I love you! We are like two lost stars alone in the heavens. Let us lock into an orbit around one another till the end of time.'
> Good luck!
> Deirdre

'That makes me want to puke,' Aunt Jetty laughed. 'Lock into an orbit around one another till the end of time! What a scream! She's as stupid as he is hopeless!'

'Oh I wish she hadn't read it in that voice of hers,' Selby thought. 'But I mustn't think about Aunt Jetty. Dear Deirdre is right — I just have to go up to her and tell her! I know she'll forgive me for being a dog. I've got to grab her and plant a big juicy kiss on her lips. Oh, how I want to lock into an orbit around Deirdre!'

It was an anxious dog who waited outside the *Bogusville Banner* office till the reporters came out. Once again they talked for a moment but, this time, they all — including Deirdre — went into The Spicy Onion. Selby waited for an hour and then two.

'I can't wait any longer,' he thought. 'I've got

to go in and tell her. I don't care if she knows that I'm the only talking dog in Australia and, perhaps, the world, as long as she knows that I love her.'

Selby crept into the restaurant and hid behind a curtain, listening to the reporters and waiting for the right moment to talk to Deirdre.

'Here goes,' Selby thought, stepping out from behind the curtain.

The reporters stopped talking and turned and looked at him.

'Hey! There's that stupid dog that came to the office the other day,' the big cigar-chomping man said. 'Get out of here, you!'

Selby was about to say, 'Deirdre, darling, I'm a dog but I love you!' and throw his paws around her and plant a big juicy kiss on her lips when suddenly there was a noise behind him. It was Aunt Jetty racing across the restaurant.

'Jock, darling,' she cried, grabbing the big man and planting a big juicy kiss on his lips. 'I love you! We are like two lost stars alone in the heavens. Let us lock into an orbit around one another till the end of time.'

Everyone stood stock still, staring in shocked silence at Aunt Jetty.

'I-I'm afraid there's been a big mistake,' the man said, drawing back. 'I'm not Jock.'

'He's not Jock?' Selby thought.

'You're not Jock?' Aunt Jetty said.

'No, that's Jock Bashem over there,' he said, pointing to the woman.

Aunt Jetty looked over at the short, plump woman with dark hair.

'You?' Aunt Jetty said. 'But you're a woman!'

'So what?' the woman said. 'Can't a woman write a sports column? You want to make something of it? Step a little closer, sister, and I'll knock your ugly block off.'

'B-But Jock is a man's name,' Aunt Jetty stammered.

'We make up names to protect ourselves from idiots like you,' the woman said, turning to the big man. 'Isn't that right, Deirdre?'

'You're Deirdre? *Dear* Deirdre?' Aunt Jetty said.

'Oh, no!' Selby thought. 'It can't be! I thought that she was him and he was her! Now everybody is somebody else and I'm not even sure who I am any more! This is a tragedy! Oh, woe woe woe.'

'Yes, I'm Deirdre,' the big man said, smiling at Aunt Jetty. 'From what you said about locking into orbit, I gather you read my column, too.'

'Oh, yes,' Aunt Jetty said, breaking out into a smile. 'I'm your biggest fan.'

'Are you really?'

'Yes, I am, and do you know something else?'

'Tell me,' the big man said, smiling back at Aunt Jetty.

'I like a man who smokes cigars,' she said. 'I smoke a few myself. I think I could lock into orbit around a good-looking guy like you.'

'Good grief,' Selby thought as he crept away into the night. 'Before these two start orbiting around each other, I think I'll streak out of here like a comet!'

O Bum, O Bum

I think the time has finally come
To write a poem about a bum
That fleshy bit behind, I mean
Around the back, so rarely seen

Poems sing of broken hearts
And lots of other body parts
There's even one about a thumb 🐾
So why not praise the humble bum?

O bum, O bum, O humble bum
Of thee I sing, of thee I hum

And why this silence, pray tell why?
Because your bum is very shy
It's almost always deathly quiet
(Depending on your type of diet)

🐾 *Paw note: I'm not sure there really is a poem about a thumb.*
S

O bum, O bum, O quiet bum
O little chum, O quiet bum

A built-in cushion, is your bott
So spare your bum a moment's thought
Then plonk yourself onto a chair
And thank your bum for being there

O thank you bum, O thank you bum
O bum, O bum, O bum, O bum.

Cloud Blaster

'Look at what your disgusting dog did!' Aunt Jetty screamed as she stepped away from something she'd trod on in the Trifles' backyard. 'Oo! Oo! Goey shoe! Horrible, horrible!'

'Not again,' Mrs Trifle sighed. 'It seems to be happening a lot these days. I don't know what's got into Selby. He never used to do these things — at least not right in the middle of our yard.'

'It isn't what's got into him,' Aunt Jetty said, wiping her shoe on a clean patch of grass, 'it's what comes *out* of him that's the problem. If he were my dog I'd just have him put down and that would be the end of this nonsense.'

'I'll have *you* put down,' Selby mumbled from his hiding place in his favourite bush. 'They think it's my fault but it's not. I only ever go to the loo in the bushland at the end of the street. It's that silly Hamish, the brain-dead sheepdog. His owners let him out and he comes in here to do his business. I've scooped a few of them up and flipped them over Hamish's fence but his owners don't seem to even notice. Speaking of noticing, I wish the Trifles would see the hole in the back fence and fix it. I've got to do something — but what?'

'It's a good thing Willy and Billy aren't here, they might have rolled in it,' Aunt Jetty said. 'That wretched disgusting dirty dog!'

'Calm down, Jetty,' Mrs Trifle said, scooping some of it up with a garden trowel.

'Get a hose, sis, and clean all this grass properly,' Aunt Jetty ordered. 'Oh, I forgot, you can't because the council won't let you water the lawn till after dark. Honestly, I don't know what this stupid town is coming to.'

'Excuse me,' Mrs Trifle said, 'but I happen to be the mayor of this *stupid town*. There is a very

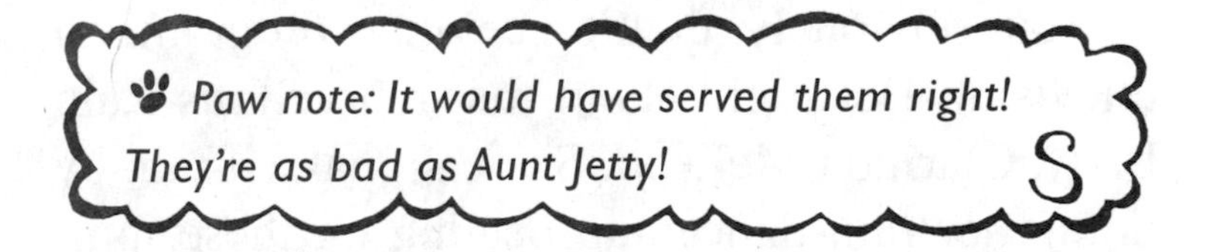

good reason why we're not allowed to use as much water as we'd like to.'

'And what good reason would that be?'

'The reservoir is nearly dry. Perhaps you haven't noticed but it hasn't rained for ages. We have to be very careful with the little water we have left.'

'Well that's not my problem. Get some water trucked in. They've got plenty of the stuff over in Poshfield.'

'We tried that,' Mrs Trifle said. 'The mayor of Poshfield won't let us have any. He says they need all of their water to keep their fountains flowing and their water-slide working and, of course, they've all got big swimming pools.'

'Can't you get a long pipe and pump some water out of a river or something?'

'Bogusville Creek has gone dry and the next river is too far away. Any other brilliant ideas?'

'I don't know. You're the mayor, do something. Make it rain, for pity's sake!'

'And how exactly would I do that?'

'You obviously didn't see that program on television last night about that marvellous Rain Lady, Clarinda McLeod. She can make it rain by doing her rain dance and beating on these tom-

tom drum thingies. She says she's made it rain in the world's driest desert.'

'I find that hard to believe,' Mrs Trifle said. 'No one can make it rain if it doesn't want to rain.'

Dr Trifle had just stepped into the backyard and was looking up at a passing cloud.

'It *is* possible to make it rain,' he said.

'Really?' Mrs Trifle said.

'Yes, people used to do what they called *cloud seeding* from aeroplanes.'

'Cloud seeding?' Mrs Trifle said. 'That sounds like they're trying to *grow* clouds from seeds or something.'

'No, they'd fly into a cloud and drop chemicals to start the cloud raining.'

'Could we do that?' Mrs Trifle asked.

'Yes, but the chemicals are very expensive and so is flying an aeroplane. I've been thinking that there must be a way to start clouds raining from down here without using expensive chemicals. Plenty of clouds come by but they usually don't drop their rain till they get to the Poshfield Hills. Hills help make it rain. Don't ask me why.'

'Then maybe we should build some hills,' Aunt Jetty said. 'But wouldn't it be easier to just get this Clarinda McLeod woman? A bit of a dance and a few taps on the old tom-toms and it'll be raining cats and dogs in no time.'

'A bucket,' Dr Trifle mumbled. 'I think that's the answer. I've got a few empty ones in the garage.'

'A bucket is the answer?' Mrs Trifle said.

'Yesssssss!' thought Selby. 'A bucket may be the answer to my Hamish problems too!'

'Yes indeedy-doo,' Dr Trifle said. 'A bucket of water. Let me explain something — a cloud is made of water. Of course the water is in tiny tiny bits like steam. Sometimes, they come together and make big drops. Big drops make other big drops and then they start to fall and you've got rain.'

'I'm not sure I follow you,' Mrs Trifle said.

'All I need to do is to get a bucket of water — maybe a few buckets of water — up into a cloud and fool the cloud into raining on Bogusville instead of waiting till it gets to Poshfield.'

'You're going to fool a cloud?' Mrs Trifle asked.

'With my Cloud Blaster,' Dr Trifle said.

'Your what?'

'My Cloud Blaster. I'll make a cannon that shoots buckets of water up into a cloud and then it'll start bucketing down, so to speak.'

'Meanwhile I'll find this McLeod woman,' Aunt Jetty said. 'She'll have it raining before you can build your silly water thing.'

'And it's payback time for Hamish, the-doo-doo-dropping sheepdog,' Selby said to himself. 'Or should I call it *poo-back*,' he added with a giggle. 'I'm going to teach Hamish and his owners a lesson they'll never forget.'

For the next few days, Selby watched as Dr Trifle built his Cloud Blaster. First the doctor took a big wide piece of steel pipe and sealed one end. Then he sawed and hammered lots of pieces of wood together to make a stand for it. It looked just like an old ship's cannon but it could point straight up at the sky.

Meanwhile, Selby was on the lookout for Hamish. Every time the sheepdog came into the yard and left something behind, Selby scooped it up and put it in a bucket he'd taken from the garage. Then he hid the bucket in the bushes.

'It's going to take forever to fill it,' Selby thought. 'I think I'll have to help it along.'

Soon Selby found himself scooping up dog — and even *cat* — droppings all over the neighbourhood till the bucket was nearly full.

'I'm almost there,' Selby thought, as he saw a strange woman arriving with Aunt Jetty. 'One more day and over Hamish's fence it goes — *hello monster poo pile*! Who is this woman?'

'Clarinda McLeod, Rain Lady,' the woman announced as Mrs Trifle opened the door. 'Your sister here says that you want me to make it rain. How much is the Council willing to pay me?'

'I-I — what?' Mrs Trifle said, turning to her sister. 'What's the meaning of this, Jetty?'

'Well you don't expect her to work for free, do you?' Aunt Jetty said. 'Give her some money, sister, so she can make it rain and fill up the reservoir.'

'But we haven't got any money for rain-making,' Mrs Trifle said. 'Besides, my husband is going to try out his rain-making gun.'

'Rain-making gun?!' the rain-maker laughed. 'That's a good one. I'll tell you what — I'm going to go right out there in front of your house and show you that I can make it rain. The first time is free. After that, you pay me, okay? Come along, Jetty.'

Mrs Trifle watched as Clarinda McLeod and Aunt Jetty unpacked their things from Jetty's car to get ready for the rain dance.

'What's happening?' Dr Trifle asked as he stepped into the loungeroom.

'Have a look. It's the Rain Lady and Jetty. They say they're going to make it rain.'

'Well I'm about to beat them to it,' Dr Trifle said. 'I've just finished making the firing thingy in my Cloud Blaster and there's a nice juicy cloud just going overhead. All I have to do now is fill the Blaster with water and *kaboom*!'

'You'd better hurry unless you want the Rain Lady to get all the credit for the rain.'

Dr Trifle dashed into the backyard and scooped three buckets of water out of the swimming pool. He then started pouring them into his Cloud Blaster.

'Hurry hurry hurry,' Mrs Trifle said.

'This is sooooo exciting,' Selby squealed in his brain. 'I hope this Cloud Blaster works! Oh, comc on, Dr T!'

Dr Trifle tipped the last bucket of water into the cannon. Then he noticed Selby's bucket, half hidden, in the bushes.

'Hmmm, what's that doing there? I must have missed one,' he said, quickly tipping it in too. 'Goodness, something smells terrible. Oh, well.'

'Oh, no!' Selby thought. 'My poo pile! He's poured all my hard-earned poo into the Cloud Blaster! I'm getting out of here! I guess I'll have to deal with Hamish some other time.'

Selby ran for the house as Dr Trifle quickly took aim with the Cloud Blaster, pointing it directly overhead and then tilting it towards the front of the house as the cloud moved slowly by.

'Stand back!' Dr Trifle yelled, pulling the string on the cannon.

Kaboom! came the blast of the cannon and a huge column of brownish liquid shot up into the cloud.

'Quickly! Into the house!' Dr Trifle yelled. 'We can watch the action from the front window.'

Outside on the nature strip, Aunt Jetty and the Rain Lady were just getting ready to dance when they suddenly looked up just in time to see the dark spray of water coming towards them.

'I hate to say it but I think that rain-gun may have worked,' the Rain Lady said. 'Look what's coming.'

'I'm afraid you're right,' Aunt Jetty said. 'But there must have been some rust in the gun because the water's all brown.'

'Why so it is,' the Rain Lady said.

Aunt Jetty and the Rain Lady were still looking up with mouths wide open when the foul-smelling liquid hit them.

'Oh, yuck!' Aunt Jetty cried, wiping it out of her eyes.

'I can't believe this!' the Rain Lady screamed, looking down at the brown stain that covered her clothes. 'Let's get out of here!'

'Why are they yelling?' Mrs Trifle said, watching the women running wildly down the street. 'Goodness, they're covered in mud. They're screaming their lungs out.'

Seconds later, a raindrop fell and then another.

'They're just sore losers, that's all,' Dr Trifle said. 'Because *I'm* the one who made it rain — not them. Hmmmm, what an awful smell.'

Selby watched as the sprinkle of rain turned into a downpour.

'You're very good, you know,' Mrs Trifle said, kissing her husband. 'I think our water problems are over — at least for now. Look, it's raining cats and dogs out there.'

Selby turned his head so they wouldn't see him giggling.

'It certainly is raining cats and dogs,' he thought. 'But raining cats' *what* and dogs' *what* I'd rather not say!'

The Tomb of the Dancing Dead

'Let's open the tomb!' said Professor Krakpott, Dr and Mrs Trifle's old archaeologist friend.🐾 'We're going in.'

A shiver ran up Selby's spine followed by another shiver and then another one that ran down. In a second he had shivers running up and down his spine.

'Sheeeeeeesh,' he thought. 'The Tomb of the Dancing Dead. I don't want to go in! But I

🐾 *Paw note: For more about the professor, see the story 'Professor Krakpott's Puzzle' in the book* Selby's Secret. S don't want to stay out here in this spooky jungle either.'

All day long Selby and the Trifles had struggled to keep up with Professor Krakpott as they walked through the rainforest.

'I'm exhausted,' Dr Trifle said finally. 'We've flown halfway round the world and . . . and now all this walking and heat . . .'

'We can't stop now, Binky,' Professor Krakpott said, using Dr Trifle's old nickname. 'We have to get into the tomb and then back to town before sunset.'

'Why do we have to hurry so?' Mrs Trifle asked, gasping for breath.

'Because the jungle comes alive at night. Deadly snakes drop from trees — and believe me, every snake in this rainforest is poisonous — spiders the size of Frisbees leap on you, vampire bats suck your blood. And then there are the leeches —'

'Leeches?' Dr Trifle said, shining his torch at his feet.

'— the size of sausages,' the professor said. 'You can't feel them creeping up your legs. Once they get a grip — well, I'd rather not think about it. And then there are the plants . . .'

'The plants?' Mrs Trifle said. 'But I like plants.'

'These are poisonous plants and flesh-eating flowers,' the professor said. 'Bump into the wrong one and it'll wrap its vines around you like an octopus. At night the jungle can swallow people up.'

'Gulp,' Selby thought. 'Poisonous snakes! spiders like Frisbees! sausage-sized leeches! poisonous plants! flesh-eating flowers! *I don't want to be swallowed up by a jungle!* Sheeesh and double sheeesh.'

'Tell us about this tomb,' Mrs Trifle said.

'It was built hundreds of years ago by the ruler of the Zolotek people, Queen Trixalotyl,' the professor explained. 'I just discovered it the other day, but there have been stories for years about a tomb they call The Tomb of the Dancing Dead. They say that on thc day of the full moon, the dead inside the tomb begin to dance.'

'But there's a full moon today,' Dr Trifle said.

'Yes, and we're going to prove that the story is a load of rubbish.'

'What if it's true?' Selby thought.

'What's if it's true?' asked Mrs Trifle.

'Not a chance,' the professor said. 'I've seen hundreds of ancient tombs, and I've never seen any dancing dead yet. Good, that's it up ahead.'

The tomb was made of huge blocks of stone with vines all over them. Little figures covered the stone door.

'Who are those people meant to be?' Mrs Trifle asked.

'They're not people,' the professor said. 'They're words written in ancient Zolotek.'

'And what Zolotek word is that picture of the largish woman?' Mrs Trifle asked.

'That's no Zolotek word. That's a picture of a largish woman — Queen Trixalotyl, the last queen of the Zoloteks.'

'I see,' said Mrs Trifle. 'Can you read ancient Zolotek?'

'No, but I know a bit of ancient Ketoloz, which I believe is similar. Let's see now . . . if I'm not mistaken this little fellow here means *in* and this one means *come* and this one means *don't*. *In come don't*. It could mean "Don't pay your income tax".'

'I think you might have it backwards,' Mrs Trifle said. 'I think it says *Don't come in*. The writing in Zolotek might be the other way about from Ketoloz.'

'Good point! Now let's open the tomb!' said Professor Krakpott. 'We're going in.'

Shivers ran up and down Selby's spine, just as they did at the beginning of this story. Dr Trifle pushed on the door but it didn't open.

'How do we open it?' Dr Trifle asked. 'It doesn't have handles like a normal door.'

'Yes, ancient tomb doors are often like that,' Professor Krakpott said.

'Maybe there's something we can push to make it open automatically,' Mrs Trifle said, 'like in those movies with the fellow with the hat and the whip.'

Professor Krakpott laughed.

'That's all movie make-believe,' he said. 'In real archaeology nothing happens automatically.'

'I still think those movies are fun. I love the way he does things in a split second to save his life. I love those really really really close calls. Do things like that ever happen to you?'

'Heavens no,' the professor said. 'Now let's look for something to prise open the door.'

While the others searched, Selby was checking his legs for sausage-sized leeches. As he did, he leant against the tomb. Suddenly the door flew open.

'Did you see that?!' Mrs Trifle exclaimed. 'It opened automatically!'

'Not really,' Dr Trifle said, looking around the entrance and then inside. 'See this? Selby must have pressed against it by accident. It's the end of a pole which goes into the tomb.'

'But how did it make the door open?' Mrs Trifle asked.

'When Selby pushed it, the pole tipped over a stone bucket inside the tomb. The bucket spilled rainwater along that ramp. Wetting the ramp allowed a big block of stone to slide along it. Then the block pulled a rope that opened the door. Simple really.'

'It sounds quite complicated to me,' Mrs Trifle said.

'And me,' Professor Krakpott said. 'But at least there's a good explanation for it.'

The professor led the way down the corridor.

'Sheeesh,' Selby thought as he followed the others. 'I don't want to go in but I don't want to stay out here either!'

Further down the corridor a wooden sign with figures painted on it blocked the way.

'Let's see now,' the professor said, reading the sign. '*Else or back go*. I guess that must mean *Go back or else*. Come along now. Follow me.'

The professor pulled the sign out of the floor and, as he did, the ground ahead of them burst open and a skeleton flew up, landing on the professor.

'Arrrgggghhhh!' screamed Professor Krakpott.

'Arrrgggghhhh!' screamed Dr Trifle

'Arrrgggghhhh!' screamed Mrs Trifle.

'Arrrgggghhhh!' screamed Selby (but they didn't hear him because they were screaming exactly the same thing at the same time).

Professor Krakpott struggled to his feet.

'It's just a skeleton,' the professor said. 'But it gave me a bit of a start. This Queen Trixalotyl obviously had a bit of a sense of humour.'

'Sense of humour?! Sheeeesh!' Selby thought. 'It's a warning! Let's get out of here!'

'Would someone please explain to me how a skeleton can jump out of the ground?' Mrs Trifle said.

Dr Trifle looked down in the hole.

'Pulling the sign out of the ground made it happen. There's sort of a catapult down there. Instead of a rubber band there's a piece of vine that's been twisted around and around like a spring. The sign pulled a pin out of the vine which then sent a shaft up and pushed a trap door open and sent the skeleton flying. Very clever but certainly not magic.'

'Come along,' Professor Krakpott said, striding ahead. 'Look, another sign. Let's see now. It says, *Will else something then don't they if and you get will death of spikes the now it for asked you.* Turning it around it says, *You asked for it. Now the spikes of death will get you and if they don't then something else will.* They're just trying to frighten us off,' he added.

'Maybe we *should* be frightened off,' Mrs Trifle said.

'Goodness me, Mrs T!' the professor said. 'If archaeologists paid any attention to signs like this we'd never go anywhere. Now come along you lot, let's see what this dancing dead nonsense is all about.'

The three of them hurried ahead with Selby just behind.

'I hate this!' Selby thought. 'If one more scary thing happens, I'm going back. They know that I have enough sense to wait for them back at the entrance.'

Just as he thought this last thought, a trapdoor in the floor suddenly opened and Selby found himself falling down a narrow shaft. At the bottom of the shaft he could see rows and rows of sharp wooden spikes sticking up.

'Help!' Selby screamed in plain English. 'The spikes of death are going to get me! Help! and double help!'

Selby clawed at the walls of the shaft but there was nothing to grip. He was upside down now, going faster and faster. In an instant he felt the first spikes part the fur on his back on their way to his flesh and then . . .

Point-of-view change warning!

We're now going to change the point-of-view of this story. This means that instead of seeing Selby, we'll see how Dr and Mrs Trifle and Professor Krakpott are getting on. You'll have to wait to find out what happens to Selby. Or you might just want to stop reading now and save yourself the terror, the agony, and the awfulness of it all.

The trapdoor closed as quickly as it had opened.

'What was that noise?' Professor Krakpott said, turning but not seeing anything.

'It sounded like a trapdoor opening and closing,' Dr Trifle said. 'Then there was what sounded like someone yelling for help. Probably just the wind outside.'

'Where's Selby?' Mrs Trifle said. 'He was right here with us a moment ago. That couldn't have been him yelling for help, could it?'

'He probably went back,' Dr Trifle said. 'He's got enough sense to wait for us back at the entrance.'

'Let's carry on, shall we?' the professor said.

. . . Selby felt the spikes of death begin to pierce his skin. Suddenly he was lying on his back, gasping for breath.

'They got me,' he thought. 'I don't feel anything. I must be dying. I don't want to die in this stupid tomb! No, no, no! My life force is draining out of me. Dr and Mrs Trifle, where are you?!'

Selby lay there, looking up the shaft.

'Oh, there are so many things I wish,' he thought. 'I wish I could fall in love just one last time. I wish I could have one final plate of peanut prawns. I wish I could roll in wet hay on an autumn afternoon. I wish I could scratch my back because it itches like the blazes. Itches? Did I say, itches? Yes, I think I did. Come to think of it, it *does* itch. I *do* have feeling! And there aren't any spikes sticking into my back and out of my tummy!'

Selby rolled onto his side and looked at what was left of the spikes of death.

'They collapsed down to nothing,' he thought. 'They must have been all rotten. They cushioned my fall! I'm alive! I'm okay! Now, that was a really really really close call!'

Nearby was a hole that opened out into a tunnel. Selby climbed into the tunnel and squinted to see what lay ahead.

'The tunnel goes down and I want to go up,' Selby thought. 'But it's the only way I can go.'

Selby walked down the tunnel, looking for a way out of the tomb.

'Oops!' he said, tripping on a piece of wood. 'What was that? And what's that rumbling noise?'

The noise got louder and louder. The dirt of the tunnel floor vibrated and suddenly a huge boulder broke through at the top of the tunnel and rolled down towards Selby.

'I must have started that rock rolling when I tripped on that wood! And now the flamin' thing's after me!' Selby screamed, as he ran as fast as he could down the tunnel. 'Help!'

The tunnel twisted and turned as it went down into the depths of the tomb. At every curve Selby looked around frantically for a way out of the path of the huge stone.

'It's gaining on me! I can't possibly outrun it!' Selby screamed. 'It's so close now that I can feel my tail brushing against it! I can't get around it or over it because it's the same size as the tunnel! It's going to squish me!'

Selby streaked around a curve. Just ahead was a stone wall. Selby let out a high-pitched scream as he hit the rock wall. In that instant the stone hit his back and his eyes began to bulge as the crushing began and then . . .

'I told you it would be boring,' Professor Krakpott said. 'What keeps us archaeologists going is that we always think that something exciting will happen. But it never does.'

'I think I hear thunder,' Mrs Trifle said. 'That rumbling. Do you hear it?'

'Yes,' Dr Trifle said. 'But it seems to be coming from underneath us, so it's probably not thunder. A slight earthquake, possibly.'

'What was that high-pitched scream?' Mrs Trifle said. 'And that terrible crashing noise?'

'I missed that,' Professor Krakpott said. 'Can't hear anything now, can you?'

'No,' Dr Trifle said. 'Not any more.'

. . . in the panic of the moment, Selby remembered something about geometry that he'd learnt on TV.

'This is a round rock,' he thought, 'about to hit a flat wall. The last place I want to be is where I am — between the middle of the rock and the middle of the wall. My only chance is to get to the outside edge of the wall where the rock will hit last!'

In a split second, Selby shot to the side as the main force of the rock hit the middle of the wall, bursting through and throwing Selby into the centre of a huge room. The rock rolled to a stop a millimetre away from him.

'That was a really really really really close call!' Selby thought. 'I've got to get out of here!'

Selby looked up and saw sunlight pouring through a narrow hole in the top of the dome. A long tree root had grown down through the hole, almost touching the floor.

'If I can get to that root,' Selby thought, 'I'll climb up and get out that way.'

Selby took a step down onto the floor and suddenly, all around the room, stone slabs revolved. Behind each one was a skeleton, suspended by a rope.

'More skeletons!' Selby said with a shiver. 'Yuck! I'll just blur my eyes and walk past them.'

Selby began to blur his eyes when strange music began to play.

'It must be the wind blowing through some primitive musical instrument,' he thought. 'It's so spooky. I'll just put my fingers in my ears.'

Just then the skeletons began jiggling up and down on their ropes.

'They're dancing!' Selby gasped. 'This is it — the Dancing Dead! The story was true! I just want to get out of he —!'

Selby was in the middle of the word 'here' when the floor beneath him collapsed and he tumbled towards the room beneath. Even in the darkness, he could see the floor of the room squirming.

'Snakes!' he thought. 'The whole floor is a mass of deadly snakes! Look! They see me coming! They're rearing up! Their mouths are wide open to strike me!'

Selby looked quickly around him as he fell. There was nothing to grab hold of, only the blocks of stone from the floor above, falling with him. As his face came closer and closer, the snakes struck out with poison dripping from their needle-sharp fangs. Selby screamed as he felt a piercing pain and then . . .

'Snakes,' Mrs Trifle said. 'I could swear someone just cried "Snakes!" Like that.'

'I heard it, too,' Professor Krakpott said. 'But I thought they said "cakes". Maybe it's one of those local people outside selling something.'

'I'm afraid it sounded like "shakes" to me,' Dr Trifle said. 'Could we go now? I'm tired of all these tunnels. I'm sure we've seen the whole tomb by now.'

'Yes, certainly,' the professor said. 'I've had enough, too. Back we go.'

And so it was that the three of them — Mrs Trifle, Dr Trifle and Professor Krakpott — made their way back towards the entrance.

'Selby?' Mrs Trifle called. 'Sellllllllllby! Where are you?'

. . . Selby realised what he must do.

'These rocks all around me are travelling just as fast as I am!' he thought. 'But if I grab one and pull myself up on top of it, it will hit the snakes first. It's my only chance!'

Selby reached over and grabbed the huge block of rock next to him with all four paws, clambering on top of it as it hit. All around him stone blocks from the floor above rained down on the snakes.

'It worked!' Selby screamed as he scrambled up to the room above and then up the dangling root to the top of the tomb. 'That's what I call a really really really really really close call!'

'There you are, Selby,' Mrs Trifle said, picking him up. 'I knew you'd be waiting here at the entrance.'

'It's been a typical archaeological day,' Professor Krakpott said to the Trifles, as they headed back along the path. 'No close calls. No split second actions. Nothing like in those movies. And no dancing dead. Dead *boring* would be more like it.'

'Maybe for you,' Selby thought. 'But certainly not for me.'

Selby's (Great) Expectations

'The reason I've asked you to come here is to tell you that Selby is now a very rich dog,' the lawyer told the Trifles.

'I'm a *what*?' Selby thought. (But he didn't say it out loud.)

'He's a *what*?' Mrs Trifle asked. (And she *did* say it out loud.)

'My client was a very wealthy woman. When she died we found this will,' Mr Jaggers said, holding up a crinkly piece of paper. 'I'll read it.'

> *To Mr Jaggers, my old friend and lawyer,*
> *When I die I would like all of my property to go to a very important little fellow. His name is Selby and he lives with his owners, Dr and Mrs Trifle, in the town of Bogusville.*

And, by the way, he's a dog. I want to give him the best life that I can. So I'm giving him and his owners the use of my mansion, Havisham House. They will be looked after by my faithful servant, Bentley, and there will be plenty of money each week for expenses. Furthermore, Selby is to be treated exactly like a person. He is to be fed the very best people food and allowed to sit at the dinner table.

'Is it a joke?' Mrs Trifle asked.

'Certainly not, Mrs Trifle. But I have no idea what was behind this. She had no family but why she would want Selby to have the use of her mansion is a mystery. She hated dogs.'

'Where is this Havisham House?' Dr Trifle asked.

'It's in the wealthiest part of Snobs' Bay.'

'But that's nowhere near Bogusville,' Mrs Trifle said. 'We'd have to move house. I'd have to quit my job. We'd miss our friends.'

'It's the chance of a lifetime,' the lawyer said. 'Your friends can email or come for visits. Havisham House is wonderful.'

'I guess if we don't like it there we can always sell it and move back,' Mrs Trifle said.

'Only if Selby agrees to sell it,' the lawyer said. 'Here's the last bit of the will.'

None of this can be changed unless Selby says so.
Remember, whatever Selby says, goes.
(signed)
Margaret Provis

'"Unless Selby *says* so"?' Mrs Trifle said. 'What "Selby *says* goes"? But Selby can't *say* anything. Are you sure that this Mrs Provis was … all there?'

'You mean, was she bonkers? I don't think so. A bit odd, maybe, but she had all her marbles. She was a remarkable woman. She made and lost several fortunes in her lifetime. At the end of her life, she was very rich again.'

'I still can't understand how this Mrs Provis even knew who Selby was,' Dr Trifle said. 'I don't think she ever lived in Bogusville. This is all so unexpected.'

Suddenly Selby's memories came flooding back.

'Margaret Provis,' he thought. 'That must have been Maggie's full name. I can't say that this was unexpected. In fact I had great expectations that something like this would happen.'

The room became all wobbly and filled with wavy lines — the way rooms do when you remember back to another time. In a second, Selby was imagining something that happened years before. There he was looking out the front window of the Trifles' house. The Trifles were away for the day and he'd just watched a TV program about first aid.

An old lady dressed in shabby clothes was walking slowly past the house. She was the woman who lived in a shack outside Bogusville.

'Poor old Maggie,' Selby thought. 'She's all alone and doesn't have a friend in the world. I wish they wouldn't call her "Maggie the Witch" behind her back. People can be so cruel.'

Selby was just thinking sad thoughts about poor people and old people and poor old people when the woman fell.

'Gulp,' Selby thought. 'Oh, no, she's not getting up! And there's no one else around! I've got to do something!'

Selby picked up the phone and was about to ring triple-O.

'But wait!' he thought, remembering the TV first aid program. 'I think I'm supposed to roll her onto her side so she can breathe properly. I'd better do that first before I call the ambulance.'

Selby dashed to the woman's side. Her eyes were closed. He put his front paws under her shoulder and started to roll her onto her side.

'You've fallen down,' he said out loud the way you're supposed to, 'and I'm rolling you onto your side.'

The woman's eyes popped open.

'What are you doing that for?! you stupid dog,' the woman snapped.

'Don't worry, I know what I'm doing,' Selby said out loud as he rolled her onto her side. 'She's really out of it,' he thought. 'She won't remember that I talked.'

'*Now* what are you going to do? you little dickens,' the woman demanded. 'You're going to bite me, aren't you?'

'No, I'm going to ring an ambulance,' Selby said calmly.

'You can't do that, you nincompoop. You're just a stupid smelly dog,' the woman cackled.

'Don't try to get up,' Selby said, dashing for the house.

Selby put on his best Dr Trifle voice on the telephone and soon the ambulance was there, taking the old woman to hospital. As they lifted her onto a stretcher, she looked at Selby.

'Listen here, dog,' she said. 'I'm sorry I was grouchy. Thanks, I owe you one. I don't like dogs but you seem okay. If I ever get my money back, I'll look after you. If I've learnt one thing in life it's this: there are times when you should help people — and stupid dogs — even if you don't like them.'

The ambulance officers looked over at Selby and scratched their heads.

'What's that dog's name?' Maggie asked them.

'That's Selby, the mayor's dog,' one of them answered.

'How'd he learn to talk?'

'Talk? Listen, lady, we've got to get you to hospital.'

'Selby,' Maggie said before they closed the ambulance door, 'you can expect to hear from me again.'

'Now I know why they call her "Maggie the Witch",' Selby thought. 'What a grouch-puss! But, you know, I think she meant that stuff about helping me.'

And so it was that Selby and the Trifles moved to Snobs' Bay, leaving their house in Bogusville empty. It turned out that Havisham House was just as wonderful as Mr Jaggers had said it was.

'The fountains and flowers are magnificent,' Mrs Trifle said to Mrs Provis's butler, Bentley, as he served tea and cakes on the verandah. 'We're so happy here.'

'And so am I,' Selby said, heaving a silent sigh.

'I'll take your dog into the kitchen,' Bentley said, 'and give him some scraps of food.'

'Scraps of food?' Mrs Trifle said. 'Oh, no, no, no. Selby is supposed to eat what we eat. It's in Mrs Provis's will.'

'With respect, madam,' the butler said, giving Selby a sideways glance, 'the old biddy is dead. She'll never know.'

'I jolly well will!' Selby thought. 'Scraps of food?! Whose house is this, anyway?!'

'I think we'd better respect Mrs Provis's wishes,' Mrs Trifle said politely.

'Anything you say, madam.'

Bentley brought the cake tray up to Selby's nose.

'That's more like it,' Selby thought as he gobbled two chocolate eclairs and sniffed a piece of chocolate mud cake.

As the days passed, Bentley was always polite to the Trifles but when they weren't looking he was terrible to Selby. Once, while Selby was sleeping, the butler trod on Selby's tail, making him jump to his feet and almost scream 'Ouch!' in plain English.

'He's smiling!' Selby thought. 'That was no accident. Owww! That hurts like the dickens!'

Another time Selby was walking past the kitchen when the butler's foot shot out and kicked him.

'What did I do to deserve a kick on the bum?' Selby wondered.

'Hey, boss,' Selby heard the cook say to Bentley. 'What did the dog do to deserve a kick on the bum?'

'I'll tell you what he did,' Bentley said. 'He inherited this house.'

'So what?' the cook asked. 'Mrs Provis had to give it to someone.'

'And that someone should have been me,' Bentley said. 'Who looked after the old grouch in the last years of her life? Not that ugly dog — me!'

'So that's it,' Selby thought. 'He's jealous. And how dare he call me ugly. I think I'm rather good-looking, to tell the truth. I'll fix him. I'm going to make the Trifles hate him so much that they'll give him the sack. *This is war*.'

Getting the Trifles to get rid of Bentley was never going to be easy. Bentley was always polite and helpful to them. They would never have believed how nasty he was to Selby.

The first battle of the war was fought in the kitchen. Selby and the Trifles had just had a meal of peanut prawns in the dining room when Selby caught sight of Bentley in the kitchen.

'Look at that guy,' Selby thought. 'He's given himself twice as many peanut prawns as he gave us. We'll see about that.'

Selby sneaked into the kitchen and grabbed a mouthful of prawns from Bentley's plate.

'You wretched dog you!' Bentley screamed.

Selby turned and ran for the dining room, gobbling the prawns as he went.

'What's wrong, Bentley?' Mrs Trifle asked.

'That dog just grabbed some food right off my plate!' Bentley screamed.

'Are you sure?' Mrs Trifle asked. 'He's never done anything like that before. Was your plate on the floor at the time?'

'I don't put my plate on the floor when I eat!' Bentley shouted. 'Your dog ate my food! You must lock him away in a doghouse or something.'

'We're not hard of hearing, so there's no need to shout,' Mrs Trifle said. 'Remember that this is Selby's house and we're *his* guests.'

'Yes, of course, I do beg your pardon,' Bentley said very politely, giving Selby a savage look.

'And that was battle number one to Selby,' Selby thought, struggling not to smile.

The second attack came when the butler was bending over in the garden sniffing a rose.

'Sorry about this, Bent,' Selby thought, looking around to make sure no one was watching.

With this, Selby leapt up, ripping a piece out of Bentley's pants.

'What the . . . !' Bentley screamed as he chased Selby across the lawn. 'I'll get you!'

And get Selby he did. In a second the furious butler had picked Selby up by the collar.

'Is something the matter?' Dr Trifle asked, as he and Mrs Trifle looked down over the balcony.

'Yes, you idiot! Your dog just tore my trousers!'

'Did he?' Dr Trifle said. 'I find that very hard to believe.'

'So what is this?' Bentley said, turning around and pointing to the tear and showing his frilly pink underpants.

'You must have caught it on a rosebush, Bentley,' Mrs Trifle said, trying not to giggle. 'Could you put Selby down? And please do not call my husband an idiot.'

'Yes, madam,' Bentley said, putting Selby down. 'I'm terribly sorry.'

'Battle number two to Selby,' Selby thought as he looked up innocently.

The next day, Bentley had just cleaned the white carpet in the library. When no one was looking Selby tracked the stickiest mud he could find all over it. He then quickly washed his paws.

'He did it again!' Bentley screamed at the Trifles. 'If you country bumpkins don't get rid of that disgusting dog, I'm out of here!'

'Bentley!' Mrs Trifle said. 'Selby's paws are perfectly clean. He can't have tracked in the mud. Some other dog must have done it. You certainly don't believe that a dog could wash his feet, do you?'

'No, ma'am,' Bentley said.

'Then either find the guilty dog or just clean the carpet again. And I'd rather you didn't call us "country bumpkins". We have lived for most of our lives in the country but we are intelligent people.'

'Yes, Mrs Trifle. I'm truly sorry.'

'Another battle for little old me,' Selby thought. 'What does it take to get this boofhead to quit?'

What it took was one last trick . . .

That evening Selby and the Trifles were sitting at the table, surrounded by wonderful food. Selby sensed that Bentley was hurrying a bit more than normal. When no one was looking Selby managed to tuck the corner of the table cloth into Bentley's belt without his noticing. Selby watched as the butler darted back towards the kitchen, dragging the table cloth and everything on it onto the floor.

'It's that dog!' Bentley screamed. 'He did this!'

'How could he have?' Mrs Trifle said. 'You obviously got it caught in your belt, that's all. It was an accident.'

'It was no accident!' Bentley screamed, purple with rage. 'That dog of yours is not a normal dog! He is cunning. He is devious! And he is evil! You're both so stupid that you can't see it! Well I've had it! I quit!'

'And the winner of the war is . . . Selby!' Selby thought. 'Sorry, Bentley, old stick, but you should always be kind to dumb animals because some of them may be smarter than you.'

Selby was still feeling proud of himself as Bentley stormed off upstairs to pack his bags.

'I guess we'll have to hire another butler,' Dr Trifle said.

'Do we have to?' Mrs Trifle asked. 'I feel uncomfortable having all these servants around. It's just not natural.'

'But it's such a big house,' Dr Trifle said. 'There's no way we could keep it running all by ourselves.'

'I've been thinking,' Mrs Trifle said. 'I don't much like it here.'

'You don't? I guess I don't like it much either. The neighbours are all too posh to be friendly. Plus I'm not doing any inventing because there's really nowhere that I can make a mess.'

'And I miss my job,' Mrs Trifle said. 'I never thought I would, but I do.'

Selby was just passing the kitchen when he heard another conversation. This time it was between the cook and the gardener.

'He's a fusspot, old Bentley,' the cook said. 'But I'll miss him. And I feel sorry for him too.'

'Why's that?' the gardener asked.

'Because of his daughter. She's sick and she needs special medicine. It's very expensive.

I don't know how he'll afford it if he doesn't keep his job.'

'What have I done?' Selby thought. 'Sick daughter? Expensive medicine? Losing his job? And the Trifles don't even like it here. Come to think of it, neither do I. It's not Bentley that should be leaving, it's us.'

Selby's mind raced as he heard Bentley close his bedroom door for the last time and start down the stairs.

'I'll go to see Mr Jaggers and tell him that I want to sell the mansion. I'll split the money between the Trifles and Bentley and then everyone will be happy. But then I'd be telling my secret. My life would be ruined! Hang on, there's another way.'

With this Selby raced to the desk in the study and got out a pen and a piece of crinkly paper. He quickly wrote a note and then crept back to where the Trifles were sitting and dropped it on the floor. It wasn't long before Dr Trifle spotted it.

'Where did this come from?' he asked.

'I don't know,' Mrs Trifle said. 'It seems to be another will. And, look, it's dated after the other one. Let me read it.'

Hiya Mizter Jaggers,
I didn't like my first will so here's another one, okay? I don't think that Selby should have the manzion after all. I know that he's a great dog, and he'z handsome and smart and wonderful and everybody lovez him, but I think the manzion should go to Bentley even if he is a pain cuz his daughter's sick and that.
So forget the other one.
Tear it up.
See ya,
Mrs Provis

'Very strange,' Dr Trifle said. 'Her handwriting certainly got worse as she got older.'

'Yes,' Mrs Trifle agreed. 'But I guess we'll have to go along with it. Poor Bentley. I didn't know his daughter was sick. We'd better stop him before he drives away.'

And so it was that later that day Bentley moved his family into Havisham House.

'I'm sure you'll be happier back in that Balloonsville place,' he told the Trifles. 'In any case — that *dog* of yours will be. I'll ask the chauffeur to drive you back.'

'That would be very kind,' Mrs Trifle said.

'Oh, well,' Selby thought. 'Easy come, easy go. I still don't like that Bentley guy very much but Mrs Provis was right: there are times when you should help people — and nasty butlers — even if you don't like them.'

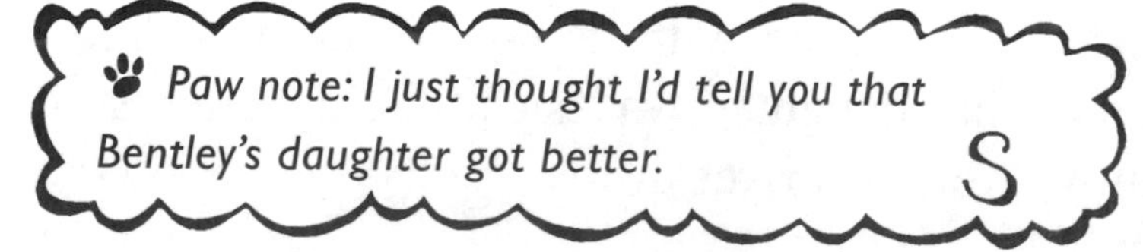

THE WORM

A worm was squiggling through the dirt
Way deep down in the garden
It bumped into another worm
And said, 'Sorry — beg your pardon.'

'You look familiar,' said our worm
'But your name I've quite forgotten . . .
Oops, now I see — you're the back of me!
I'm talking to my bottom!'

NEAT STREETS

'Jump into your work clothes,' Mrs Trifle announced on Saturday morning. 'Today is CUB Day.'

'CUB Day? I've never heard of CUB day.'

'It stands for Clean-Up Bogusville Day, silly.'

'Oh, I completely forgot,' Dr Trifle said. 'I'm busy today. Can't we clean up Bogusville another time?'

'Sorry, everything's organised for today,' Mrs Trifle said. 'Besides, we could be about to win the Neat Streets award. The judge will be inspecting Bogusville tomorrow morning.'

'Neat Streets award? What's that?'

'You know when you drive into a town there's often a sign that says it has won the Neat Streets award? Bogusville has never won.'

'So what makes you think we'll have a chance this year?'

'Because I've heard that they want to give the award either to us or to Poshfield.'

'But Poshfield is full of rich people, and their streets are always neat,' Dr Trifle said. 'They'll win for sure.'

'Yes, but I was just talking to the mayor of Poshfield, Denis Dorset. He didn't mention the award. I don't think he knows that the judge is coming tomorrow. They've just had a footy match and they still haven't cleaned up all the litter.'

'I hope you didn't tell him.'

'Good heavens no! Now will you hurry up and finish breakfast so we can get to work? I'm so excited about this! It's almost Christmas, and winning the Neat Streets award would be a lovely Christmas present for Bogusville.'

'I love it when people work together to make things better,' Selby thought as he lay under a tree watching the Bogusville volunteers picking up bits of rubbish by the roadside. 'I'd love to help,' he said with a sigh, 'but I can't, of course. I guess I'll just have to watch.'

The volunteers threw rubbish bags filled with litter onto the back of a truck. Each time the truck was filled, it took a load to the tip. All day long the people of Bogusville walked along every street and through every park, removing rubbish.

'I'm exhausted,' Dr Trifle said at the end of the day. 'I'm so sore from bending over. I don't think I'll ever be able to straighten up again.'

'It's good for you, dear,' Mrs Trifle said. 'It'll make you fitter. And look how nice our streets are now.'

'They're much better,' Dr Trifle admitted, 'but they're not perfect. The bottles and the big pieces of cardboard are gone but there are still lots of little scraps.'

'We can't possibly pick up everything,' Mrs Trifle said. 'What worries me more is that the judges usually give the award to a town that makes an extra effort.'

'What sort of extra effort?'

'Like polishing statues and decorating lampposts. We haven't done any of that because there's just no time. The main thing is that Bogusville now has much neater streets than Poshfield.'

'I beg your pardon?' a voice said.

Mrs Trifle turned around to see none other than Denis Dorset, the mayor of Poshfield, stepping out of the back of a long black limousine.

'Marvellous job,' he said, throwing away his cigar and almost hitting Selby. 'For a very, well, *ordinary* town Bogusville looks cleaner than ever.'

'Denis!' Mrs Trifle exclaimed. 'What are you doing here?'

'I'm on a very peculiar mission. We need a little bit of help using one of your good husband's inventions.'

'What did I do now?' Dr Trifle asked.

'You invented a wonderful machine some years ago — the Vacu-Shred Clean Machine. Do you remember?'

'Oh, yes. A street-cleaning machine with a difference,' Dr Trifle said, smiling to himself. 'I gave away the plans but no town could afford to build one — not even Bogusville — because it was too expensive.'

'Nothing's too expensive for us,' the mayor of Poshfield said. 'We had one made. But we're having trouble getting it going. Perhaps you could help us.'

'Why, yes, of course.'

'Good, because we have a bit of a litter problem and we need a quick clean-up in time for the Neat Streets inspection tomorrow.'

Mrs Trifle looked at Dr Trifle and Dr Trifle looked at Mrs Trifle and Denis Dorset looked at both of them and Selby looked at all three of them. Mayor Dorset was the only one who was smiling.

'We'll see you straight away in Poshfield, Doctor, shall we?' he said, hopping back into his limo and speeding away.

'What a hide that man has!' Mrs Trifle cried. 'Why did you agree to show him how to work the street-cleaner?'

'I had to. It's the duty of every inventor to show people how to use their inventions.'

'Well, you're a very good man,' Mrs Trifle said. 'And I'm sure it's the decent thing to do. But it will probably cost us the Neat Streets award.'

'He's such a good man,' Selby thought. 'But sometimes I think he's too good for his own good.'

The streets of Poshfield were as clean as ever, except for the litter along the main street left over from the footy match. Dr and Mrs Trifle and Selby drove up to the council garage. Outside was the new Vacu-Shred Clean Machine. Denis Dorset had the door open and was looking at all the foot pedals and levers.

'It's really quite easy,' Dr Trifle said, getting into the driver's seat as Denis Dorset sat beside him and Mrs Trifle and Selby sat behind. 'Push the starter button.'

Selby could barely hear the engine start but in a second the truck was driving along the main street of Poshfield. Dr Trifle pulled a lever and a long arm which looked like a huge elephant's trunk came out of the top of the truck.

'This is the Snorkel Arm,' Dr Trifle explained. 'Point it towards the rubbish and it will do the rest.'

With this, the Snorkel Arm shot over to one side and sucked up a chocolate bar wrapper. Then there was a faint whirring sound.

'That's the shredder,' Dr Trifle went on. 'The shreds get blown into the back of the truck. Then you drive it to the tip, pull the Blower Lever, and everything blows back out again. Simple. Want to drive it?'

'Not just yet,' said the nervous mayor. 'Keep going for a while and then I'll take over.'

Dr Trifle drove the street-cleaner through town, cleaning one side of the street as he went.

'Careful on the turns,' he said, edging the machine around very slowly. 'The wheels are close together so that it can get down narrow streets. This makes turning a bit tricky. Want a go?'

'Just do a bit more and then I'll take over.'

Dr Trifle drove the Vacu-Shred back to the garage, cleaning the other side of the street as he went.

'Now it's your turn,' he said.

'Me?' the mayor said, rubbing his hands together. 'Why should I? The Neat Streets judge is only going to inspect the main street and you've cleaned it beautifully.'

'How do you know the judge will only inspect the main street?' Mrs Trifle asked.

'Let's just say that a little birdy told me,' Denis Dorset said with a giggle.

That night Selby lay awake furious at Poshfield's mayor.

'That dirty Denis!' he thought. 'He tricked Dr Trifle into cleaning up Poshfield! This isn't fair! Oh how I wish I could get him back for that! Hey! I've got it!'

Selby sneaked secretly and silently out of the house and ran through the deserted streets of Bogusville. Soon he was in Poshfield, standing outside the council garage.

He quietly raised the garage door, crept into the driver's seat of the street-cleaner and started the engine. In the headlights he could see a stack of red, white and green banners hanging on the wall. They said:

CONGRATULATIONS, POSHFIELD!
WINNER OF THE NEAT STREETS AWARD!

'Why, you sneaks!' Selby thought. 'You haven't won it yet! This is what I think of your banners.'

Selby steered the Snorkel Arm towards the banners. One by one he sucked them up, sending long strips of shredded banner into the back of the truck.

'That was fun!' he squealed. 'Now to drive this baby over to Bogusville and do a little extra cleaning. Ready, steady, and off we go!'

Selby drove through the deserted streets to Bogusville. He steered the Vacu-Shred Clean

Machine along Main Street sucking up little bits of rubbish everywhere.

'There, now we at least have an equal chance,' Selby thought. 'I'd better get the machine back.'

Maybe it was because it was the middle of the night. Maybe it was because Selby was exhausted from a long day. But one thing was for certain — Selby forgot what Dr Trifle had said about turning the Vacu-Shred around.

Selby spun the wheel and suddenly the machine lurched to one side, tipping up and nearly turning over.

'Yikes!' Selby screamed as he fell against the door. The door flew open and Selby grabbed for the nearest thing he could to keep from falling out — the Blower Lever. Suddenly there was a whirring and a blowing as the Vacu-Shred lurched from side to side down the street.

'It's like riding a bucking horse!' he squealed. 'I can't hang on any longer!'

Selby flew through the air, landing in a ditch. He jumped to his feet to see the Vacu-Shred weaving wildly, blowing shredded paper through the Snorkel Arm and into the night sky.

'Come back!' Selby screamed, running after

the out-of-control machine as it spewed red, green and white strips.

Selby ran down the middle of the street after the speeding machine. Now the trees and poles and wires along the streets were covered in strips of paper.

'I've ruined everything,' he moaned as the driverless shredder shot away towards Poshfield. 'All that work that everyone did, and now Bogusville doesn't have a hope of winning. Oh, woe woe woe.'

Selby dragged himself back home and lay down, exhausted. He awoke the next morning to the sound of Mrs Trifle's voice.

'There's been a disaster!' she cried. 'We're finished!'

'What sort of a disaster?'

'The police found your Vacu-Shred lying in a ditch on the road to Poshfield. It appears that *someone* used it to spread litter all along the main street of Bogusville.'

'Denis Dorset!' Dr Trifle said. 'I cleaned his streets and now he's littered ours!'

'We don't know that he did it,' Mrs Trifle said. 'And, because we can't prove it, we shouldn't even be thinking it. It does look highly suspicious. Come along, I guess we'll have to face the music.'

'I beg your pardon?'

'The Neat Streets judge has already been to Bogusville and now she's inspecting Poshfield to decide who the winner will be. We all know who's going to win, but I'm the mayor so I have to go to the ceremony.'

Dr and Mrs Trifle and the town council waited at Bogusville Town Hall as Denis Dorset drove up in his limousine. With him was the judge, an old woman with white hair.

'This is Mrs Trifle, the mayor of Bogusville,' Denis said, grinning from ear to ear. 'Mrs Trifle, this is the Neat Streets' judge — Dolores Dorset.'

'Dolores Dorset?' Mrs Trifle said, shaking the woman's hand. 'Did you say Dorset?'

'Yes, I'm his mother,' Mrs Dorset said. 'But don't let that worry you. I've had a good look at Poshfield and Bogusville and I'm going to be as fair and honest as I can be,' the woman added, looking around at the strips of paper hanging from trees and wires. 'I've made up my mind. This year's Neat Streets award goes to . . . Bogusville!'

Denis Dorset's jaw dropped.

'Mum! How could you?!' he cried. 'This town's a mess! Look at all that rubbish up in the trees!'

'Nonsense, Denny,' Mrs Dorset said. 'Bogusville is very neat. Just as neat and clean as Poshfield. And those red and green and white Christmas streamers show that they made that little extra effort I always look for.'

'Mum, Mum,' Denis blubbered. 'How could you do this to me? What did I do to deserve this?'

'Stop your nonsense this instant, Denis!' the old woman scolded. 'I'll tell you what you did to deserve this — you never cleaned your room when you were young. You lied, you cheated, and you made every excuse to get out of cleaning your room. And who had to clean up after you? I did! Me, your poor mother. Well now we're even. And I'll tell you something else,' she said, smiling as brightly as Mrs Trifle, 'right now I feel kind of good.'

'So do I,' Selby thought, smiling to himself as tears rolled down Denis Dorset's face. 'And I guess Poshfield won't need those Neat Streets banners after all.'

SELBY'S NEW YORK ADVENTURE

'I just love your little town!' New York police officer Lieutenant Larry Laws said to Mrs Trifle. 'I come here every year to relax.'

'It's not so relaxing when you live here,' Mrs Trifle said. 'But at least we don't have as much crime as you do in New York City.'

Selby looked up from where he was lying.

'This guy's got to have the most exciting job in the world,' he thought. 'I'd love to be a New York cop. All those car chases and blazing guns and screaming sirens. It must be sooooo much fun!'

'Speaking of crime,' the policeman said, turning to Dr Trifle. 'You're an inventor — I wonder if you could make a cam-collar.'

'Don't you mean a cam*corder*?' Dr Trifle asked.

'No, I mean a cam-*collar* — a mini TV camera that could be clipped to a dog's collar. We could use it in our NYPDCC program.'

'I beg your pardon?'

'The New York Police Department Clever Cops program. Gone are the days of car chases and blazing guns and screaming sirens. Crims are getting smarter so these days we try to outwit them.'

'It sounds a lot safer,' Mrs Trifle said.

'Yes, but it's not as much fun,' Lieutenant Laws sighed. 'I kind of miss a good car chase with blazing guns and screaming sirens. One thing we do now is use more dogs.'

'What sort of dogs?' Mrs Trifle asked.

'Dogs like your Selby are very useful when they're trained.'

'Selby? Useful? Really?' Mrs Trifle said. 'I thought police dogs had to be fierce.'

'Fierce schmierce. This guy's a great judge of dog,' Selby thought as he struggled not to smile. 'What clever cops need are clever dogs — like me.'

'The thing about Selby,' Larry Laws said, 'is

that he's sort of a *nothing* dog — just an average sort of dog that nobody notices.'

'Hey, hang on,' Selby thought.

'We notice him,' Mrs Trifle said. 'He's not a nothing dog to us. We love him very much.'

'I didn't mean to be rude,' the police officer said. 'The point is that he'd be the perfect dog to tail a crim.'

'To what a what?'

'To tail a criminal — to shadow someone.'

'Oh, you mean to *follow* someone,' Dr Trifle said.

'Exactly. Right now we're after a woman called Barbara Bransky. "Babs" used to work in a bank. After she retired, they realised that she'd stolen one million dollars, just a little bit at a time.'

'Why don't you arrest her?' Dr Trifle asked.

'Because we can't prove it. And we can't find the money. She's got it hidden. We think she's about to get the money out of hiding and then leave the country but every time we try to follow her, she spots our tail.'

'I see,' Dr Trifle said, checking to see if there were any spots on Selby's tail. 'So if you put this cam-collar on a dog and have the dog follow her then you could watch from a safe distance —'

'Exactly!' Larry Laws interrupted. 'When she locates the loot, we pounce. Do you think you could make a cam-collar?'

'I think so,' Dr Trifle said. 'I'll also make a tiny ear-piece to go in the dog's ear so that you could give him directions like "Stay!" and "Sit!" and things like that.'

'Dr Trifle, you are one heck of an inventor!' the policeman exclaimed.

For the rest of the day Dr Trifle hammered and sawed pieces of metal and then attached lots of pretty-coloured electrical bits. When he was finished, he spray-painted it to match Selby's collar and clipped it on. He turned on the switch and then put the tiny ear-piece in Selby's ear.

'There you are, Larry,' he said. 'Let's give this thing a go.'

Selby watched as Dr Trifle turned on a TV. Sure enough, the camera was looking at everything in front of Selby.

'That's fantastic!' the police officer said. 'When I get back to New York we'll start training a dog to use it.'

'How will you do that?' Dr Trifle asked.

'I'm not sure. We could slip a dog biscuit in

someone's pocket for starters,' the policeman said. 'Then the dog would follow them. He'd have to be a dog that could follow directions.'

'Why don't we try it out on Selby?' Mrs Trifle asked.

'Oh, no, it would be far too tricky for an old dog like him,' the policeman said. 'You know the old saying, "You can't teach an old dog new tricks".'

'I could teach him a new trick or two,' Selby thought. 'Why doesn't he just give me a go?'

'Why don't we just give Selby a go,' Mrs Trifle said. 'He might surprise us.'

And surprise him, Selby did. All day long Dr Trifle and Larry Laws watched as Selby followed one person after another through Bogusville. He kept well behind so he wouldn't be noticed. Whenever the person stopped, Selby would stop too. He listened on the ear-piece as Dr Trifle and Larry Laws said 'Stay!' and 'Stop!' but, of course, he knew exactly what he was doing.

'This dog of yours is absolutely amazing!' the policeman exclaimed. 'He can follow directions even before we give them! Can I borrow him and take him to New York?'

'Yes, okay,' Mrs Trifle said. 'But we will worry about him.'

'Don't you worry your little heads,' the police officer said. 'New York's Clever Cops will take good care of him.'

'Oh boy, oh boy, oh boy!' Selby thought. 'This is it! I'm off to New York to be a clever dog for the Clever Cops!'

A few weeks later Selby found himself walking through the streets of New York City.

'This is so exciting,' Selby thought. 'I've never seen such tall buildings! Wow!'

Ahead of him Babs Bransky weaved her way through the crowds. She kept looking back and every time she did, Selby stopped or hid behind something. On and on she went — crossing streets and then crossing back, walking up an alley and then turning back.

In his ear-piece, Selby could hear the police officers.

'This is it,' Larry Laws said. 'Babs is going for the money this time. We know that she's packed up the stuff in her apartment. I figure she's ready to skip the country. But we'll get her this time.'

'Yeah, Larry, that Aussie dog of yours is doing

a great job! He seems to know just what to do.'

'That's because we slipped a Dry-Mouth Dog Biscuit in Babs' pocket. Apparently he loves them.'

'That'll be the day,' Selby thought.

Selby watched as the woman stopped in front of an old building. She stood in the entrance, looking around. Suddenly, she turned and went in.

'It's in that building!' he heard Larry Laws say. 'She's got it hidden in there somewhere. Get a patrol car over there right away!'

'I'll have one there in about three minutes.'

'Why so long?'

'The closest car we have is on 42nd Street. They're on their way.'

'Tell them not to use the siren. I don't want to scare Babs off.'

'So what am I supposed to do?' Selby thought. 'Maybe I'd better go in after her.'

Selby raced across the street and into the building. He looked around. The building was empty. He could hear the woman's footsteps on the stairs above him. Very quietly, he made his way upwards until he could hear a door open.

'This dog is incredible!' he heard Larry Laws say. 'He's followed her all the way to the roof. She must have a hiding place up there. This is going to make things easy.'

Selby waited a minute and then went through the door and out onto the roof. Sure enough, there was Babs Bransky prising the cover off a metal vent. One by one, she took out ten big wads of money.

'That's it!' Selby squealed in his brain. 'That's the million dollars!'

'That's it!' Selby heard Larry Laws say. 'That's the million dollars! Where's that car?'

'It's stuck in traffic on 38th.'

'But she'll get away!'

'So what am I supposed to do?'

'I've got to do something to stall her,' Selby thought.

The woman was picking up the first bundle of banknotes when Selby came up beside her. She turned around quickly.

'Oh, it's only a dog,' she sighed. 'You frightened me. What are you doing up here? Whose dog are you? I wonder.'

The woman was about to start putting one of the bundles of money in a bag when Selby rubbed against her.

'You want a pat, do you?' she said sweetly. 'Of course you do. Come here, sweetums.'

'Look! She's patting him!' he heard the policeman say. 'I hope she doesn't notice the collar-cam.'

'Me too,' Selby thought. 'They'd better hurry up and get here.'

'You're a real sweetie,' the woman said, giving Selby a big cuddle. 'I'd love to have a dog like you. They wouldn't let me have one in my apartment. Now that I'm moving to the country, I think I'll get a dog. How about you? Want to come with me? Of course not. You're someone else's dog and I'm sure they love you. And you love them too, don't you, snookums?'

'Where's that car?!' Selby heard Larry yell.

'Keep your shirt on, boss. The guys'll be there in two minutes.'

'You heard the woman, she's heading for the country! If she gets away with the money, it's going to be your fault!'

Selby rubbed up against the woman. She seemed to forget about the money and patted him and cuddled him more. There was a sweetness to her voice as she told him about her years of working at the bank, about living with her old mother until she died, about never being able to afford any of the things that she wanted, and about never being able to have a pet.

'The poor woman,' Selby thought as tears formed in his eyes. 'She's had such a terrible life and now it's going to get worse. (Sniff.) She won't get the money and she'll go to jail. (Sniff.)'

'The car is here,' he heard the police officer say.

'Tell them to wait at the entrance and nab her when she comes out,' Larry Laws said. 'That stupid woman is still playing with the pooch. What a jerk!'

'Hey, hang on,' Selby thought. 'She's not a jerk. She's lovely. And she likes me too. Okay, so she stole a few bucks. She's still a nice person.'

The woman was still stroking Selby when he reached up with his paw and turned off the cam-collar.

The last thing he heard was, 'Hey, we're losing contact. She must have discov —'

'Okay, Babs,' Selby said. 'Time to go.'

The startled woman stepped back.

'You're a talking dog!' she said. 'I can't believe it!'

'You'd better believe it because it's true.'

'But I've never seen a talking dog before. What kind of dog *are* you?'

'I'm an Australian dog but don't worry about that. Just scoot.'

'What are you talking about?'

'I'm talking about you getting out of here quick-smart. Leave the money and run, Babs! The cops are waiting for you downstairs.'

'How do you know that?'

'I know a lot,' Selby said. 'And believe me, I know what I'm talking about.'

'But I didn't see them. Usually I see them following me.'

'They've outsmarted you this time.'

'So I'll just leave the money and walk out. They can't do anything because they didn't see me with the money.'

'Don't try it. They've seen you already.'

'How'd they do that?'

'There's a tiny TV camera on my collar,' Selby said, showing it to her. 'I've been following you and they've been watching. But I like you. You're sweet. I don't want you to get caught, okay?'

The woman shook her head.

'You are a clever dog,' she said. 'So how do I get out of here without getting caught?'

'Climb over that wall to the next roof and then go down the fire escape to the alley,' Selby said. 'I'll pretend I'm you and distract them.'

'How will you pretend you're me?'

'I'll put on your voice,' Selby said, putting on the woman's voice.

'A talking dog that does impressions,' the woman said. 'Now I've seen everything. Okay, I'll do what you say.'

'Hurry!'

Selby watched as the woman reached for a packet of money.

'And don't you dare touch that money!' Selby said.

'Okay, okay,' the woman said. 'How about just ten dollars for a taxi?'

'All righty but only ten.'

The woman shoved the money in her handbag.

'Thank you, doggy,' she said as she climbed over to the next roof.

Selby waited till she'd started down the fire escape and then called down the stairs.

'Officers! It's me, Babs!' he said, using Babs' voice. 'I give up! Come and get me!'

In an instant the police came rushing up. They burst through the door with guns drawn.

'Freeze!' they yelled. 'Hey, she's gone! Where'd she go?!'

The other police officer looked over the edge of the building.

'Look! She's down there! She got away again!'

'But she didn't get the money,' the other police officer said. 'Look, it's all here in these ten bundles,' he said, counting them out. 'One, two, three, four, five, six, seven, eight, nine, oops! That rascal! She made off with a bundle! She got away with one hundred thousand dollars!'

'A hundred thousand smackeroos!' Selby thought. 'That sneak! I let a sweet little old lady outsmart me! So much for Selby the clever, crime-fighting canine.'

STICKS AND STONES

'Ooooooooooooaaaaaaaaaaaah!' Selby screamed. 'Shu-Kik-Shin! Shu-Kik-Shin! Kik! Kik! Kik!'

Selby's feet flew out in all directions in a blur — like an ice-skater losing his balance. After a few seconds, he fell flat on his face on the floor.

'This is supposed to be relaxing — but I'm exhausted!' he thought as he looked at Mrs Trifle's book, *Shu-Kik-Shin, The Warrior's Ancient Art of Relaxation.* 'Maybe I'm not doing it right.'

Selby turned back to the front of the book.

'Let's start with *The Pose of the Reed* again.'

Selby put his paws on his hips like the woman in the picture. Then he swayed back and forth.

'Simple dimple,' he said, turning the page. 'Now for *The Pose of the Poppy*.'

Selby put his front paws on his neck and stretched his head upwards.

One after another Selby moved through all of the poses.

'So far, so good,' he thought as he turned to the second last page. 'Now for *The Pose of the Stick*. Back legs together, front legs up. Okay, head back, eyes closed, empty the mind. Empty the mind? How can I empty my mind? I can't just stop thinking. When I close my eyes I think even *more* than I did with them open. What's next?'

Selby turned to the last page.

'*The Pose of the Stone*,' Selby said, hunching down and curling up. 'Now the power of the cosmos is supposed to flow through my body. I can't feel any power flowing through anywhere. I just feel sore, that's all. Okay, this is it — stand up, kick like crazy and scream.'

'Oooooooooooaaaaaaaaaaaah!' Selby screamed. 'Shu-Kik-Shin! Shu-Kik-Shin! Kik! Kik! Kik!'

'Goodness! What was that noise?' Mrs Trifle said, coming in the door followed by a young girl.

'I didn't hear anything,' Prunella said. 'Are you sure it wasn't the wind?'

'I guess it must have been, Prune,' Mrs Trifle said, using Prunella Weedy's nickname. 'Have you brought your book with you?'

'I'm sorry, I forgot,' Prunella said.

'Prunella! How do you expect me to help you with your reading when you keep forgetting your book?'

The girl suddenly burst into tears.

'Prune, darling, you shouldn't be this upset,' Mrs Trifle said, putting her arm around the girl. 'Is something bothering you?'

Prunella nodded. 'There's this girl at school who keeps picking on me.'

'What girl?'

'Chantelle-Anne Blande. She calls me "Zipper-mouth" because I've got bands on my teeth. And she calls me "Seedy Weedy".'

'Well that's silly,' Mrs Trifle said. 'There are lots of kids with bands on their teeth. And Weedy is a perfectly nice name. Just remember: "Sticks and stones will break my bones but names will never hurt me".'

'She doesn't just call me names. She makes fun of everything about me.'

'Like what?'

'I'm skinny and my knees are knobbly and my hair sticks out everywhere — not like hers — and my eyes are different colours and —'

'She's being silly. Have you told your teacher what's happening?'

'No, I don't want to be a dobber,' Prunella said, bursting into tears again. 'I told Mum but she just says to ignore her. But how can I? She keeps saying things about me. She says, "You have a face like a flower — a *cauli*flower." And "Is that you, Zipper-mouth? Or is it someone imitating a stick-insect." Things like "I see that you've got something on your mind today — ooops, sorry, it's only your hat."'

'Those aren't very funny,' Mrs Trifle said.

'No, but it makes the kids laugh at me.'

'Your mother is right — ignore her. If you ignore her long enough, she'll stop.'

'I just wish I could say things back. I've tried but I can never think of what to say. I looked up some funny insults on the Internet. There's this comedy thing by Gary Gaggs, the comedian.'

'Yes, I know Gary. He's a friend of ours.'

'Well he's got these joke insults. But when Chantelle-Anne starts in on me I panic and forget them. All I can say is "I know you are but what am I!" and stuff like that. The kids only laugh more. I just feel like beating her up but I've never beaten anyone up before. Besides, she's bigger than me.'

'Beating her up is not the answer, Prunella. Don't even think about it.'

'I hate this Chantelle-Anne girl,' Selby thought. 'How could she be so cruel to poor old Prune? She's such a sweet girl. She even saved my life one time.'

'I'm scared to go out for recess,' Prunella said. 'What can I do?'

Suddenly Mrs Trifle noticed the book that lay open on the floor.

'This could be your answer,' she said.

'Is it a book of insults?'

'No, it's a way that ancient warriors used to make themselves calm before a battle. If you're really calm, nothing will bother you.'

'Does it work?'

'I don't know. I'm only up to page four. Here, borrow it. See how you go.'

'Hang on,' Selby thought. 'I was just making myself calm too! Oh, well, maybe it'll work for her. But I reckon it would be much much better just to get that horrible Chantelle-Anne girl back. That's what I'd do — if I could only think of how. Hmmm.'

For the next week Selby's brain raced around in circles like racing cars on a speedway as he tried to think of a solution to Prunella's problem.

'If she could only remember Gary Gaggs' insults,' Selby thought. 'But I know what she means about forgetting things when she panics.'

Suddenly, a light came on in Selby's brain.

'Dr Trifle's cam-collar!' he thought. 'The one I used in New York! It's perfect!'

Selby searched through a box of Dr Trifle's old inventions till he found the tiny device. He removed the tiny ear-piece and tiny microphone, putting the camera part back in the box. He grabbed the big microphone and turned it on.

'Testing, one, two, three,' he said. 'Great! It still works perfectly!'

Selby put the device in an envelope marked 'Prunella' along with a note. He left it on Prunella's doorstep just before the girl came home from school and then hid in the bushes across the street.

'Good,' he thought. 'I can see her from here and she can't see me.'

Selby watched as the girl opened the envelope. She read Selby's note out loud.

'"If you want to get back at that Chantelle-Anne girl, then pin the microphone to your shirt and put the ear-piece in your ear." Hey! What's going on here?' she said looking around. 'Who left this here?'

After a while, Prunella did as the note said.

'Now to turn on my mike,' he thought. 'Hello, Prunella. Can you hear me?'

'Yes, I can hear you. Who are you?'

'This is Dr Trifle,' Selby said, doing his perfect Dr Trifle imitation.

'Where are you?'

'Never mind about that, Prune. You and I are going to play a little trick on Chantelle-Anne.'

'We are?'

'We are. Mrs Trifle tells me that she's been picking on you.'

'All the time,' Prunella said.

'Well you and I are going to make her regret that she ever picked on you. Would you like that?'

'Yes, of course,' Prunella said, still looking around.

'There's one condition — nobody's allowed to know about this, okay?'

'If you say so. But why are you hiding, Dr Trifle?'

'Never mind about that,' Selby said. 'Tomorrow, before you go out for recess, pin the microphone on your shirt where it doesn't show and put the ear thingy in your ear. Don't let anyone see you do it. Then let Miss Smartytrousers say something and I'll do the rest.'

'But I don't understand.'

'You will, Prunella, you will.'

That evening when the Trifles had gone to bed, Selby booted up their computer and printed out the Funny Insults page of Gary Gaggs' Gagg Bag web page.

The next day Selby hid in the bushes outside the school as the kids came out to play. He watched Prunella step nervously out the door.

'Okay, Prunella,' Selby said again. 'Whatever happens, keep smiling.'

'Here she comes now,' Prunella whispered. 'I'm scared.'

'Don't be.'

Selby watched as the bigger girl stood in Prunella's way. The other kids gathered around to watch.

'Well, well, well,' Chantelle-Anne said. 'Did anyone ever tell you that you've got a pretty little head? It surc is *pretty little*! Ha ha ha.'

Selby could hear the kids laughing. He quickly thumbed through Gary Gaggs' funny insults.

'That was pathetic, Prunella,' he said. 'Tell her this: As a wit, you're not half bad, Chantelle-Anne. In fact you're a *half-wit*.'

Selby listened and watched as Prunella delivered the line perfectly, throwing back her head at the end of it and laughing. All the kids laughed along with her.

'Good one, Prune,' Selby said. 'Now let's see what she says.'

'You're so thin,' Chantelle-Anne said, 'it would take two of you to make a shadow.'

Again the kids laughed as Selby searched through his page.

'That's even more pathetic,' he said. 'Hang in there, Prunella. Here's one: Excuse me, Chantelle-Anne, but is that your head or is your neck blowing bubble gum?'

Once again Prunella said the line like a real comedian. This time the kids laughed even harder.

Chantelle-Anne's smile began to fade as she said: 'Yeah, well is that a pimple between your ears or is it your face?'

'Pimple schmimple,' Selby said. 'She's losing it. Hit her with this one — I used to think you were scatter-brained but now I know you don't have enough brains to scatter.'

'Oh yeah!' Chantelle-Anne said angrily. 'And you're so skinny you have to run around the shower to get wet!'

'Keep smiling,' Selby said. 'You're winning.

Here you go: You know, Chantelle-Anne, if ignorance is bliss, you must be the happiest girl alive.'

'What? I don't get it?' Chantelle-Anne said.

'She doesn't get it, Dr Trifle.'

'Who are you talking to, skinny minnie?'

'Don't talk to me!' Selby said. 'Here's one she'll understand: Looks aren't everything, Chantelle-Anne. In fact, in your case they aren't *anything*!'

With this the kids roared with laughter and Chantelle-Anne was fuming.

'Do you want to lose five kilos of ugly fat?' she screamed. 'Then cut off your head!'

'Hopeless,' Selby mumbled. 'Tell her this: You'll go far, Chantelle-Anne — and the sooner the better.'

Suddenly a light rain began to fall. But no one seemed to notice. And so it was that a tiny raindrop made its way down into Prunella's ear.

'What's that ugly growth on your neck?!' Chantelle-Anne shouted. 'Oh, sorry, it's your head!'

'Ridiculous,' Selby said. 'Hey, I'm enjoying this. Here's one for her: The only way you'll ever make up your mind is to put lipstick on your head.'

'What?'

'I said, the only way you'll ever make up your mind is to put lipstick on your head.'

'I can't hear you,' Prunella said again. 'Something's gone wrong.'

'Oh, no,' Selby thought. 'The ear-piece has got rain in it. It's not working! I can hear her but she can't hear me!'

Selby watched as Chantelle-Anne started to smile again.

'You're so stupid you'd stay up all night studying for a blood test,' Chantelle-Anne said.

Panic spread across Prunella's face.

'That's what *you* think!' she snapped.

'Prunella, no! Just walk away! Don't say things like that! Oh, no, she still can't hear me!'

'You know why things go in one of your ears and out the other, Zipper-mouth?' Chantelle-Anne said. 'Because there's nothing to slow them down! Ha ha ha. But you do have a soft heart. Unfortunately you've got a soft *head* to match. Ha ha ha! I'll bet you sing like a nightingale. You certainly have a *bird* brain! Ha ha ha!'

'Walk away, Prunella! She's killing you!'

Selby watched in horror as Prunella suddenly put her hands on her hips and started swaying in the wind. The kids fell silent and watched. So did Chantelle-Anne.

'She's doing *The Pose of the Reed*!' Selby thought. 'She's trying to calm herself down! Now they'll really laugh at her! What's she doing now?'

Selby watched as Prunella did *The Pose of the Poppy* and then all the other poses from Mrs Trifle's book. By the time she got to *The Pose of the Stick* and, finally, *The Pose of the Stone*, the kids were laughing their heads off.

'This is terrible!' Selby cried to himself. 'Why did Mrs Trifle give her that book?!'

Suddenly Prunella rose to her feet and gave a huge yell: 'Oooooooooooooaaaaaaaaaaaaaaah!' she screamed. 'Shu-Kik-Shin! Shu-Kik-Shin! Kik! Kik! Kik!'

With this her feet shot out like bullets, hitting Chantelle-Anne and sending her rolling in the dirt. The kids gasped as Prunella drew a deep breath and pressed her knuckles to make them crack.

'No! No! Don't kick me again!' Chantelle-Anne pleaded. 'I'm really sorry, Prunella, honest I am.' By now there were tears rolling down the big girl's face. 'I won't pick on you any more, honest! Please don't kick me!'

'Okay,' Prunella said calmly. 'But if you do, that was only a little taste of what I'll do to you. Do you understand?'

'Please don't do it again, please. I promise I won't pick on you ever again.'

With this Prunella turned and walked calmly back into the school. The kids cleared the way. Selby could hear them clapping.

'I don't know what to think about that,' Selby said, shaking his head. 'All I know is that life is full of surprises. And if it isn't, my name's not Selby, the talking dog.'

'It's working again, Dr Trifle,' Prunella said. 'What was that about a talking dog?'

'Oooops, nothing, Prune. Just talking to myself.'

Madame Mascara's Passion Potion

'Hair of dog!' announced Madame Mascara, the former fortune-teller turned cosmetics millionaire. 'I need hair of dog.'

'I beg your pardon,' said Mrs Trifle.

Selby watched as Madame Mascara dashed past Mrs Trifle and into their house, carrying a large iron pot.

'I am making a potion,' Madame Mascara explained. 'And there are a few things I need.'

'A what?'

'A potion. A brew, drink, a bit of this and that all mixed together. It's right here in *Ye Olde Booke of Potions and Spelles*,' Madame Mascara said, holding up an old book. 'I'm short a few of the ingredients. I thought you might have some.

One of them is *hair of dog*. I could just clip a clump of fur from little dogums here.'

'Hey, hang on!' Selby thought. 'How would she like someone to clip a clump from her?'

'Tell me more about this potion,' Mrs Trifle said.

'It's a *love* potion,' Madame Mascara explained, waving her long purple fingernails in the air. 'Dab a bit on you and everyone who smells it will get all huggy huggy and kissy kissy.'

'Do you really believe there's such a thing as a love potion?'

'Of course I do! One whiff and people go crazy with love. And love *is* a kind of craziness.'

'I don't know,' Mrs Trifle said. 'I love my husband and I love Selby but I don't go crazy over them.'

'No, my darling Mrs Trifle. You *love* them. Being *in love* is completely different. People who are *in love* will climb the highest mountain or dive to the bottom of the sea. They will do anything for the person they're in love with. They just go mad mad mad.'

'Why do you want to make people go mad mad mad?'

'I will put love potion in one of my House of Mascara perfumes. I will call it *Madame Mascara's Passion Potion*. Everyone will flock to buy it. They will pay anything! And I'll be filthy rich. Of course I'm already filthy rich but this will make me even filthier rich. I can't wait! Turn to page XXV in the book and let's get mixing!'

Mrs Trifle opened the book as Madame Mascara put some water in the pot.

'I'm only putting in a tiny bit of water because I want it to be a very potent passion potion,' she said. 'I'm not going to heat it because heat will make it weaker. Okay, what's the first ingredient?'

'It says *wing of bat*,' Mrs Trifle said. 'I'm afraid I don't have any of that.'

'Then we'll substitute something else,' Madame Mascara said. 'A good cook always substitutes things. How about licorice? That's black and gummy like a bat's wing.'

'I have some sweets in a jar from when the girls' hockey team was over the other day. I think I have a licorice jelly bean.'

'Chuck it in,' Madame Mascara said.

Mrs Trifle threw the jelly bean into the pot and then read the next ingredient on the list — *eye of newt*. What's a newt?'

'Oh, it's just one of those slimy little lizardy things. How about a piece of sago, that looks like a newt's eye.'

Mrs Trifle threw a piece of sago into the pot and watched as Madame Mascara stirred it in with a big wooden paddle.

'This is ridiculous,' Selby thought. 'The woman's an idiot.'

'This one's easier,' Mrs Trifle said. '*Slime of snail*. But we've got rid of our snails.'

'Slime of *slug* will have to do,' Madame Mascara said. 'I've got some of that.'

Madame Mascara whipped a jar out of her pocket, scooped out a gob of goo and flicked it into the pot.

'What's next?' she asked.

'A *clutch of cobwebs*,' Mrs Trifle said reading on.

'Got that, too,' Madame Mascara said,

throwing a handful of sticky spider web into the pot. 'Next?'

'A *pinch of ragweed*,' Mrs Trifle said. 'I've never seen ragweed growing around Bogusville.'

'Neither have I,' Madame Mascara said, pulling a few small flowers out of her pocket. 'So we'll have to make do with flannel flowers.'

'But ragweed is a completely different plant to a flannel flower.'

'Yes but think of it this way: rags are made of cloth and flannel is a *kind* of cloth, so it's close enough. What's next?'

'*Hair of wolf*,' Mrs Trifle said. 'We don't even have a wolf at the zoo.'

'Easy peazy,' Madame M said, grabbing a clump of Selby's fur from the end of his tail and clipping it off so quickly that he didn't have a chance to blink. 'This is why I wanted hair of *dog*. A wolf is just a kind of dog, after all. Now to give it a good stir.'

Selby jumped to his feet and spun around, looking at his tail.

'I'll have to wait ages till it grows back!' he thought. 'I should have got out of here when that fortune-telling fruitcake came in! What a waste of good fur — this love potion stuff is never going to work anyway. Especially not with all the wrong ingredients.'

'Now for the most important part of all: the magic words,' Madame Mascara said, leaning towards the book and chanting:

> 'Witchity wotchity finicky funk
> Tinkery tankery wobbly wunk
> Dab this brew on a homely soul
> And everyone shall see a gorgeous hunk'

'Oh, dear. Gorgeous hunk,' Madame Mascara said. 'I think this potion is meant for a man. Dr Trifle! Could you come here?'

'I'm in the middle of something,' Dr Trifle sang out from his workroom. 'Would you mind coming here instead?'

Madame Mascara quickly snatched up the pot and stepped forward, not noticing Selby still staring at the bite out of his tail fur. And as she did so, she tripped, spilling the pot.

'Oh, no!' Selby thought as he jumped to his feet. 'I've been dabbed! What am I talking about? — I've been drenched! Get this guck off me!'

'Selby!' Mrs Trifle cried, grabbing a towel and beginning to dry him. 'You poor dear.'

'Oh, drat,' Madame Mascara mumbled. 'All that work and now I'll have to start all over again.'

'What's the commotion about?' Dr Trifle said as he appeared in the doorway. 'And what's that strange smell?'

'We spilled love potion on Selby,' Mrs Trifle said.

'Love potion? But there isn't any such thing as a love potion.'

Selby saw a strange look come into Dr Trifle's eyes. At first Dr Trifle was amazed, then dazed and then his eyes were completely glazed.

'My goodness,' he said. 'Selby does look good today. He's downright handsome — handsomer than I've ever seen him before. Selby, what's happened to you?'

'Hey, he thinks I'm handsome,' Selby thought.

Selby turned to see the glazed look come into Mrs Trifle's and Madame Mascara's eyes.

'He looks rather . . . fetching,' Madame Mascara said, taking a deep breath.

'Fetching?' Selby thought, as he caught sight of himself in the mirror. 'I'm just me — I just look normal . . . actually, I think I look rather good today. Hmmm, but there is something weird about mirrors.'

By now, Madame Mascara and Dr and Mrs Trifle were kneeling on the floor, hugging Selby and stroking his fur.

'Oooooooooh Selby!' Mrs Trifle moaned, clutching him closer.

'Selby, you are absolutely beautiful!' Dr Trifle said, wrapping his arms around Selby's middle.

'This is kind of nice,' Selby thought. 'I guess that Passion Potion works after all. Lucky me.'

'You're the most gorgeous hunk I've ever seen!' Madame Mascara squealed, pressing her face to his. 'I'm going to sack all of my models and put you in my next *House of Mascara* perfume catalogue. Just you you you! You are the most scrumptious dog in the . . . the universe! When people see your picture they'll buy everything!'

'Hey, hang on!' Selby thought as he tried to wriggle free. 'This is getting a bit much. Their eyes were glazed and now they're crazed! They've all gone gaga! Oh, well, it should wear off in a minute or so.'

Just then Selby's eyes saw the lines at the bottom of page XXV in *Ye Olde Booke of Potions and Spelles*.

When the spell is said and the potion applied
And it has well and truly dried
It shall forever with thee reside.

'*Forever with thee reside*. What does that mean? Oh, no! Once it dries it's on me forever! It never wears off! I've got to have a shower — quick!'

Selby struggled free and then turned towards the bathroom only to have the three of them dive in front of him.

'I'll never make it!' he said, dashing out the door. 'My only hope is to get to the showers at the sportsground!'

'Please come back!' they screamed after him. 'Don't ever leave us!'

In a second, Selby was around the corner, over a fence and running through bushland towards the sportsground.

Suddenly the branches of the bush parted in front of him and there, staring with grinning faces, were the dreadful duo, Willy and Billy. Before Selby could jump sideways, their hands shot out and grabbed him.

'I've got you now, you poo poo . . . you stink-face . . . you . . .' Willy began.

Selby could see the boys' angry faces turn to surprise. And if that wasn't bad enough, there was a crash in the bushes behind him. Suddenly the hideous shape of their mother, Aunt Jetty, towered over them.

'Put that filthy dog down!' she boomed.

'He he he's . . . pretty, Mummy,' Willy said, hugging Selby.

'Can I have him, Mummy?' Billy said, clutching Selby's legs. 'I want him!'

'You can't have him, stinky!' Willy said, pulling Selby by the collar. 'He's mine! I love him!'

'He *loves* me?!' Selby thought. 'Did he say he loves me?! This passion potion *is* potent! Help! They're choking me!'

In a second the two boys were screaming and crying and pulling Selby in different directions.

'Boys! Stop that! Let go of him!' Aunt Jetty screamed. Suddenly she sniffed the air. 'Goodness! I see what you mean. Who would have believed that such an ugly mutt could turn into a gorgeous hunk. Let me at him, boys.'

Before Selby knew it Aunt Jetty's lips were burrowing into his fur.

'Moo-ah! Moo-ah! Mooooooooooo-ah!' she said, kissing him all around his head. 'You gorgeous creature you! Get away, boys! He's mine!'

Aunt Jetty lifted Selby into the air with Willy and Billy still clinging to him.

'They're going to pull me to pieces!' Selby screamed in his brain. 'I've got to get loose even if I have to —'

Selby didn't finish his thought. Instead he opened his jaws as wide as he could and clamped them down on Aunt Jetty's ear.

'Yowch!' she screamed, grabbing her ear and letting Selby fall to the ground. 'How could you do this? you great big beautiful thing you! Or was that a love bite? Bite me again, gorgeous!'

Selby quickly shook Willy and Billy free and was off and running again.

'There it is! — the sportsground!' he thought. 'And the girls hockey team is out on the field so I can nip into the shower block and wash this glurp off me.'

In a second Selby was standing in the shower and had started seriously soaping.

'This just has to work,' he thought. 'It's my only chance.'

Selby turned off the shower and gave himself a big shake. Just then he heard the unmistakable tiny voice of Prunella Weedy saying, 'Selby?'

Selby looked around to see the whole girls' hockey team standing and watching him, their noses sniffing the air.

'I've been sprung!' Selby thought. 'I may have got rid of the Passion Potion but now they all know that I'm not just an ordinary non-talking, non-showering dog!'

'Selby?' the shocked girl said a little louder. 'You're . . . you're the most beautiful being I've ever seen.'

'Oh, no! I didn't get rid of the Passion Potion after all!' Selby thought as he saw the glazed eyes all around slowly turning to crazed eyes. 'Let me out of here!'

Suddenly a camera flashed.

'I'm going to rip down all my posters of Todd Delvane and cover my walls with pictures of you, Selby,' a girl screamed.

Suddenly Selby was snatched and stroked by seventeen supple pairs of hands.

'You are my true love!' one of the girls cried.

'Back off!' another girl said. 'He's *my* true love!'

'No, he's not! He's mine!' another girl screamed, raising her hockey stick.

In a second there were punches, and screaming, and much pulling of hair as the girls rolled around in a mass on the ground.

'They're mad!' Selby thought as he squiggled through a forest of kicking feet. 'I've got to get out of here!'

'There he goes! After him!' the girls screamed.

Selby was running down the street with both hockey teams in hot pursuit along with Willy, Billy, Aunt Jetty, and now the Trifles and Madame Mascara. Everywhere people stopped to stare at them and then joined in.

'What a dog!' people cried and, 'Come back here, you wonderful hunk!' as more and more people joined in the chase.

'How is this going to end?!' Selby wailed to himself. 'I can't keep running forever!'

It wasn't a human who finally stopped it, it was Hamish the-not-very-bright-but-always-cheerful sheepdog. Selby turned for a second and saw that look in Hamish's eyes. Just then Hamish grabbed him by the leg and brought him crashing to the ground. And in a second, there was a huge pile of screaming people in the middle of Bogusville.

'This is it!' Selby thought. 'I've been stampeded! I'm a done dog!'

A police siren sounded and the crowd suddenly parted, leaving Selby lying there looking up at Sergeant Short and Constable Long.

'What's got into you people?!' Sergeant Short shouted.

'It's him,' Postie Paterson said, pointing to Selby.

'Who, Selby?' Sergeant Short said. 'What's he done?'

'You're not looking at him. Have a look.'

Selby watched as the policeman's eyes slowly glazed over.

'Oh, great,' he thought. 'Here we go again.'

'Selby,' Constable Long said. 'I never noticed it before but you are really beautiful. I think . . . I think I'm in love with you.'

'Oh, no!' Selby thought. 'I'm about to be kissed by a cop!'

'Hang on a tick!' Sergeant Short yelled. 'He's mine!'

'No, he's mine!' someone in the crowd yelled and the crowd moved forward.

'It's my only chance! I've got to speak or I'm dead!' Selby thought, clearing his throat. 'Stop!'

he yelled in plain English. 'Stay right where you are! Get a grip on yourselves!'

The crowd stopped.

'Selby,' Mrs Trifle said, 'you spoke.'

'Yes, I spoke,' Selby said. 'I know how to talk — and read and write — but never mind about that. You've all gone crazy because of Madame Mascara's perfume.'

'What perfume?' Madame Mascara asked, looking completely confused.

'Your Passion Potion,' Selby said. 'You spilled it on me. It works. Only it works *forever*! I don't want to go through life having people cuddling me and kissing me. I'm not a *doll*, you know, I'm a *dog*. *Now* do you love me?'

'Yes, we do!' the crowd roared.

Selby looked around at all the faces.

'This is going to be mean and cruel and nasty,' he thought, 'but I've got to do it. It's the only way. Okay,' he said out loud, 'if you really love me then you have to do as I say —'

'We'll do anything for you, Selby!' someone cried.

'Okay, here are the rules . . .'

Selby had just finished telling them that no one was allowed to pat him for more than a minute and only when he wanted them to when suddenly he saw their faces begin to change. Their crazed looks suddenly turned to glazed looks and then to dazed looks and then to amazed looks and suddenly they were scratching their heads and wondering what was going on. Selby stopped talking.

'What are you all doing here?' Sergeant Short asked.

'It's wearing off,' Selby thought. 'The Passion Potion is wearing off! It didn't last forever! It must be because Madame M used the wrong ingredients! And now that the spell is broken, they don't remember that I talked! I'm a free dog! Oh joy, oh joy!'

'What am I doing here?' Madame Mascara said, as she wandered off, following other people who were wandering off.

'And what's Selby doing here?' Mrs Trifle asked, picking him up. 'Phew! Oh, Selby, you smell very strange. Come along and let's give you a good bath.'

'Oh, isn't life wonderful,' Selby thought as the Trifles carried him home. 'The Trifles are the most wonderful people in the world. I love them and they love me. But I hope nobody ever falls *in love* with me again.'

My Itch Attack

One day I had an itch attack
And bent my leg behind my back
And scratched and scratched and
scratched and scratched
And scratched and scratched and
scratched and scratched
And scratched and scratched and
scratched some more
(Then all my fur fell on the floor!)

SELBY SURVIVES

Selby sensed that a storm was coming.

He could feel it in his bones. He could smell it in the wind. He could see huge clouds building up over the ocean. And he'd heard it on the weather forecast. Well he sort of heard it.

While the TV director of *Outcast Island* was counting the coconuts with votes scratched on them to see who was going to be voted off the island, Selby stood on the beach and could barely hear a radio on the boat that was moored nearby. What he heard was:

Crackle crackle. '(mumble mumble) . . . warning . . .' *crackle* '(mumble) . . . cyclone . . .' (mumble mumble) '. . . waters north of Point (mumble) . . . ' *crackle crackle* '. . . warning . . . high winds and high seas . . .'

'Gulp,' Selby thought. 'I wonder if that was north of Point *Vertical*? That's where we are! I don't envy these *Outcast Island* people if they're stuck on this island in a storm. I'll be okay because I'm heading for the mainland with the TV crew.'

Selby watched as the director read off the names from the coconut shells.

'We have a loser,' he announced. 'I'm afraid it's Mandy-Lou. Sorry, Mandy-Lou, I know how much you wanted to win a million dollars. But you've had a good time, haven't you?'

The woman wearing an *Outcast Island* T-shirt walked to the centre of the circle. There were tears in her eyes.

'I'm really sorry to go because — hey — I thought I was going to win the money. But — hey — it's okay. You can still lose and be a winner. I'm a winner because — hey — I love each and every one of you. You'll all be my dearest friends for life, okay?'

'Woo woo, Mandy-Lou!' the others cheered. 'We love *you*, Mandy-Lou!'

Mandy-Lou turned to the director. 'How was that?'

'That's just fine, Mandy-Lou.'

'Okay so my contract's finished, right?'

'You're a free woman, Mandy-Lou.'

'Is the camera off?'

'*Cut!* It is now.'

'All right you sleaze-balls!' Mandy-Lou screamed. 'Thanks a bunch for voting me off the island! And after all I did for you! You voted against me, didn't you, Sharlene. You with that make-up to cover the wart on your nose — you witch!'

'Mandy-Lou, it's time we went back to the mainland,' the director said, pulling the screaming woman towards the boat.

'Get your filthy hands off me, you creep!' Mandy-Lou yelled. 'And as for you, Chuck, it's off between us! Don't ever ring me! You're a liar and you're short! Goodbye shrimp!'

'Mandy-Lou, relax, it's over. You'll be on a plane home tonight.'

'Lying cheating nincompoops!' Mandy-Lou yelled, spitting on the ground. 'I thought we were friends but you're only in this for the money! I hope I never see any of you again!'

'Wow!' Selby thought. 'I had no idea that these *Outcast Island* people hated each other so much.'

The director picked Selby up and began wading out towards the boat along with Mandy-Lou and the TV camera and sound people. The nine outcasts stood watching. Then one of the women spoke.

'Would it be okay to leave Dingo here for the night?' she asked.

'I guess so, Holly,' said the director. 'We don't have to send him back to Bogusville till tomorrow.'

'Dingo?' Selby thought. 'Hey, hang on, that's me! I don't want to be left here overnight! Especially not with a storm coming! Help!'

'Oh, thank you,' Holly said, taking Selby out of the director's arms. 'I just want him to keep me company.'

As the TV crew sped away, the director yelled out, 'You'd better make shelters for yourselves! It looks like rain!'

Selby's mind went back to the day when Mrs Trifle saw an ad in the Bogusville Banner for a dog to be in the TV series *Outcast Island*.

'I love that show!' he thought. 'I love the way they work out puzzles. I love the campfires, and secret caves, and notes that are burnt around the edges! I love everything about it! Maybe they'll choose me and I'll get to win a million smackeroos.'

Mrs Trifle emailed a photo of Selby and the TV company loved the look of him. They came to talk to the Trifles.

'We just want him for two days,' they said, handing the Trifles a cheque. 'Don't worry, we'll take good care of him.'

'This is going to be sooooo much fun,' Selby thought.

The next day Selby was on the island. There, a team of make-up artists dyed his fur to make him look like a dingo. Then they put him in some nearby bushes and started the cameras.

'Look! There's one of those dingoes!' he heard one of the outcasts whisper. 'He's after our food!'

'Quick! Make a big fire to keep him away!' another outcast whispered back. 'Where are the guys?'

'*Cut*!' the director called. 'That was great, girls.'

'Is that it?' Selby wondered. 'Did they bring me all the way here just to pretend I was a dingo for a couple of seconds? I guess they did.'

Selby watched all afternoon as one of the outcast teams had to figure out how to get to the top of a palm tree to find a secret map. The other team was doing an enormous crossword puzzle in the sand using huge letters that they'd found in a treasure chest. A TV helicopter circled overhead to take pictures. Finally, just before voting Mandy-Lou off the island, the outcasts had to eat raw birds' eggs, sandworms and a handful of ants while the TV crew, and Selby, helped themselves from platters of delicious food.

But now the day was over and Selby and the outcasts were alone on their tiny island.

'Hey, everyone,' Holly said to the others. 'I've got an idea. Let's all make a shelter together.'

One of the others gave her a dirty look.

'Make your own shelter,' he snapped.

'You just want us to help you, don't you?' another outcast said.

'No, I don't. I was just thinking —'

'Think again, Hol,' one of the other women said. 'Maybe you can get the dog to help you.'

'Hey, guys,' someone else said. 'Tomorrow let's vote Holly off the island.'

'Good idea,' one of the men said.

'But that's not fair!' Holly sniffed. 'You're ganging up on me.'

'Oh, go play with your dog,' someone said.

Holly carried Selby into the palms and sat down.

'You're a darling,' Holly said, cuddling Selby. He could see the tears forming in her eyes. 'I really hate these people,' she went on. 'They're all so spiteful and nasty. They can't even pretend to be nice. All they want is the money. Tomorrow they're going to vote me off the island and guess what?'

For a split second Selby forgot himself and almost said, 'What?'

'I'll tell you what,' Holly said. 'I don't care if they *do* vote me off the island. I'm sick of this. I only wanted to come here so I'd be noticed and maybe I'd get somc acting rolcs.'

Selby could see the others collecting anything they could to build their shelters — palm fronds, bits of wood, pieces of bark. On the horizon, the storm clouds were getting bigger and darker.

'Thanks for the cuddle, Holly,' Selby thought. 'But you'd better get a wriggle on. I don't fancy lying around all night in the rain.'

'I guess I'd better make a shelter,' Holly mumbled. 'I'm not much good at this stuff but then neither are the others.'

Selby watched as Holly searched for building materials.

'I guess this is it,' she said, dumping an armload of things on the ground.

'This is what?' Selby thought. 'What kind of a shelter does she expect to make from a piece of bark, a handful of grass, three chocolate bar wrappers and a rubber thong?'

Holly studied her small pile of material for a minute, grabbed the piece of bark, lay down and covered her head with it.

'Goodnight, Dingo,' she said.

'Holly, this is stupid,' Selby thought. 'You're sweet but you'll never be a survivor.'

Selby ran around the island looking at the shelters the other outcasts were building. There were bits of plastic and piles of dried leaves and even some boards that had been washed up on the beach.

'They're almost as bad as Holly's,' Selby thought as he remembered a TV program he'd seen about making shelters in the bush. 'And that sky is looking worse and worse.'

Selby tore along the beach, digging here and there when he saw something poking out of the sand. In a few minutes he'd found a length of rope and a long section of fishing net.

'This is good strong stuff,' he thought as lightning lit up the sky. 'Now lots of palm fronds and some big strong branches.'

Selby dragged his materials back to where Holly lay sleeping. He jabbed one end of the sticks into the ground and then tied their tops to the trunk of a palm. After an hour, Selby was exhausted.

'Now why couldn't they all get together and do something like this,' he thought.

Selby put the fishing net over the wooden frame and tied it to two nearby palms. Then he started poking palm leaves through the net.

'Now that's what I call a proper shelter,' he thought as he crawled inside and lay down next to the sleeping girl.

Soon the wind was blowing steadily and the rain began. Holly sat up and looked around her.

'Goodness, look what I made,' she said. 'And I don't even remember doing it.'

Then she lay down again and began to snore.

'You don't remember it because *you* didn't make it,' Selby said out loud. 'I did! You and

your friends are hopeless! You're supposed to be survivors but you're nothing but a bunch of selfish losers. You spend all your time fighting with each other when you could be helping each other out. People who work together will be the real survivors and don't you forget it. I'm leaving tomorrow. I have more important things to do with my life than to look silly on TV and hang around with a bunch of morons like you.'

Holly sat up and stared in the darkness at Selby. There was a strange expression on her face. She was frowning but smiling a tiny smile at the same time. The rain was bucketing down now and the wind was howling through the trees.

'Is that you, Dingo?' she said. 'Were you just talking to me?'

Selby was about to say, 'I certainly was,' when there was a voice behind him.

'Holly, can we come in?'

One by one the other outcasts crawled into Selby's shelter. The wind howled and thunder boomed. No one spoke. Minutes passed and then hours but in the morning, when the sun rose, Selby's shelter was still there. One by one the outcasts crawled out. In the distance the TV boat was speeding towards the island.

'Thank you so much, Holly,' one of the women said. 'Where did you learn to make a shelter like that?'

'I was so upset last night that I don't remember a thing,' Holly said.

'Well you saved our lives and we've decided not to vote you off the island today.'

'Oh, thank you,' Holly said.

All of a sudden Selby saw Holly's strange expression again.

'I have these words in my head,' she said.

'What words?'

'I don't know. Thoughts. Things I have to say.'

'Well then go ahead — speak.'

'I just wanted to say that I think you're all hopeless. Listen to me and listen carefully. You're supposed to be survivors but you're nothing but a bunch of selfish losers. You spend all your time fighting with each other when you could be helping each other out. People who work together will be the real survivors and don't you forget it.'

'Is that it?' one of the men asked.

'No, there's one more thing. I'm leaving tomorrow. I have more important things to do with my life than to look silly on TV and hang around with a bunch of morons like you.'

Everyone was quiet for a moment. Suddenly they began cheering.

'Is everybody there?' the director yelled from the boat. 'Thank goodness you're okay. We didn't have any warning of that storm.'

'Look at that! There's Selby,' Dr Trifle said to Mrs Trifle a few days later when they were watching TV. 'They've made him up to look like a dingo but he still sort of looks like Selby.'

'This'll be the last episode,' Mrs Trifle said.

'Really? Why's that?'

'Because the outcasts have all quit.'

'Do you mean none of them wants the million dollars?'

'Apparently not. They didn't explain why, they just voted themselves off the island. The TV people are very upset.'

'It doesn't make sense,' Dr Trifle said.

Selby looked up from where he was lying.

'It makes perfect sense to me,' he thought, as he admired himself in his dingo make-up. 'But I have to admit that *I* don't look so silly on TV. In fact, I think I look quite handsome.'

Santa Selby

'What would you like for Christmas?' Dr Trifle asked. 'I've bought a few presents for you but I'd like to get one more thing.'

'Don't get me anything else,' Mrs Trifle said. 'You've probably already bought too much.'

'No, I haven't. It would be impossible to buy you too much. Is there still something that you really really want?'

'There is one thing. Remember the beautiful vase that Willy threw at Billy last year?'

'Only he didn't throw it at Billy,' Selby thought. 'He threw it at *me*! the little terror.'

'Do you want another one just like it?' Dr Trifle asked.

'Yes, that would be lovely.'

'Your sister, Jetty, ought to buy it,' Dr Trifle

said. 'Her sons broke it. She's so careful with her money, that sister of yours. You always buy her nice presents, and what does she do? Last year she gave you one of those plastic toys from a breakfast cereal packet. A little robot with wheels — only one of the wheels was already broken.'

'Now, now,' Mrs Trifle said. 'We mustn't think that way. *Giving* is the most important thing.'

'Yes, of course,' Dr Trifle said. 'Sorry, I just forgot myself for a minute. Where would I find a vase like the one you had?'

'The only possible place would be in the department store over at that new shopping mall at Poshfield. But today is the day before Christmas and the mall will be a madhouse. Why not give me a vase for my birthday instead?'

'Are you sure you don't mind waiting that long?' Dr Trifle asked.

'Of course not, dear.'

'Oh, aren't the Trifles lovely,' Selby thought. 'They're just the most wonderful people in the world. They don't even hate those monsters Willy and Billy for breaking that vase.'

Selby lay there thinking about how much he wanted to give Dr and Mrs Trifle a present. He remembered when he first learnt to talk and how the first thing he was going to do was to say 'Merry Christmas' to the Trifles. But he also remembered why he didn't talk to them. He was afraid they'd put him to work around the house. And worse — he might be sent off to a laboratory to be studied by scientists. Or he might be dognapped and held for ransom.

A cold shiver ran up Selby's spine as he thought of all the close calls he'd had. But soon the cold shiver turned into a warm, Christmassy feeling again.

'Dr Trifle might not like to mingle with Christmas crowds but I do,' Selby thought. 'I think I might just go over to Poshfield Mall and mingle to the sound of *Jingle Bells*.'

That morning Selby found himself running along a country road and then over fences and fields to the new mall in Poshfield.

'Wow!' he thought, as the glass doors opened and he started up the escalator. 'Look at all the shops! Look at the big Santa Claus on his sleigh hanging from the ceiling! And look! There's his reindeer too! Oh, I love Christmas!'

'Hey, you!' a voice behind him said. 'Hey, dog! Get out of here!'

At the top of the escalator, a man in a guard's uniform stood with folded arms.

'What's this about?' Selby wondered as he started back down the Up escalator, dodging the people coming up. 'I'm not hurting anyone.'

Selby turned to see the man bounding down the other escalator.

'Uh-oh! This guy means business,' Selby thought as he ran faster.

Selby and the guard got to the entrance at the same time.

'Out! Out!' the man said, clapping his hands and stamping his foot.

'Out, out, yourself,' Selby thought as he ran out the door. 'It's not fair. I wasn't going to touch anything. I was just mingling.'

On the way home, still feeling awful about what had happened, something popped into Selby's head.

'The dog suit!' he thought. 'I'll climb under the house and get my dog suit. If I wear that and stand on my hind legs, no one will suspect there's a dog inside.'

A short while later Selby was back at Poshfield Mall, mingling and wearing the dog suit. This time the guard gave him a strange look but then smiled.

'Merry Christmas,' Selby said out loud.

'And a merry Christmas to you too, sir,' the guard said back. 'What a nice dog suit.'

Everywhere that Selby went people looked at him and smiled.

'Look at the man in a dog suit,' a little girl said. 'Look, Mum!'

'I'm not a man in a dog suit,' Selby laughed. 'I'm a *dog* in a dog suit. Merry Christmas.'

'Merry Christmas Mr Dog Man,' the girl said.

'This is more like it,' Selby thought. 'Oh, they're playing *Jingle Bells*. I love all that dashing through the snow business. It cools me off just to hear it.'

Selby was in the Glassware Section when something caught his eye.

'That's it!' he thought. 'It's just like the vase that Willy and Billy smashed! And it's on special! And it's the very last one! Oh, how I wish Dr Trifle was here so he could buy it for Mrs Trifle. Even better — oh, how I wish I had some money so I could buy it for her myself! Why oh why did I come here?'

Selby felt a tap on his shoulder. This time it

wasn't the guard in the guard's uniform but a man wearing a name tag that said *Store Manager*.

'Where have you been?' the man demanded.

'What do you mean?' Selby asked.

'I'll bet you were off entertaining at some kid's birthday party or something?'

'No, I wasn't,' Selby said.

'Don't lie to me, Jack,' he said, grabbing Selby by the sleeve. 'Come on, it's Santa Time. There are already fifty kids waiting.'

'Hey! Let go of me,' Selby said. 'There's been a mistake.'

'It was my mistake to hire you,' the manager said. 'Where have you been for the past two days?'

'But I'm not Jack,' Selby pleaded.

'Don't play games with me,' the manager said. 'Do you want to get paid in advance? Is that it?'

'Pay? I mean, did you say pay? In advance?'

'I'll tell you what,' the man said, getting out his wallet, 'you'll get half now and half when you've talked to the kids.'

Selby looked over at the vase. A woman had just picked it up and was looking at it.

'Forget the money,' Selby said, 'I'll take that vase instead.'

'That vase? But that only costs —'

'I don't care,' Selby said. 'I want it. Get it for me or there's no deal.'

'It's yours,' the manager said, snatching it out of the woman's hands. 'Now get into the Santa suit.'

Selby followed the manager into a back room. There was a Santa suit piled on a chair.

'Well? What are you waiting for? Get into it.'

Selby waited for a moment but the manager wasn't going to leave him alone. So he started pulling on the bottom of the suit.

'Aren't you going to take off the dog suit?' the man asked.

'No, I think I'll leave it on.'

'Leave it on? Why?'

'I'm cold,' Selby said, as he pulled on the top part. 'All this air-conditioning. Besides, I'll look fatter and jollier with both suits on. I'll be a better Santa Claus.'

'But how about that dog face?'

'The beard will cover it,' Selby said.

'Okay, suit yourself,' the manager said, suddenly laughing out loud. 'Get it? *Suit* yourself? Oh, I'm funny even when I'm not trying.'

'One more thing,' Selby said. 'Would you mind gift-wrapping that vase?'

'I guess I could do that.'

And so it was that Santa Selby listened as one child after another told him about the Christmas presents they wanted.

'I want a doll,' a little girl said.

Behind her, Selby could see the girl's mother nodding.

'Yes, I think Santa could bring you a doll,' he said. 'Ho ho ho. Merry Christmas.'

'I want a truck,' a boy said.

'A toy truck,' Selby said, looking over at the boy's father, who was nodding. 'I think we could arrange that.'

'I don't want a *toy* one,' the boy said. 'I want a *real* one. If you're really Santa Claus you can get it for me.'

'But my elves don't make real trucks,' Selby said. 'They're too short. They only make toy ones.'

'Okay,' the boy said. 'I'll have a toy one. That's okay.'

'I want a puppy,' a girl said.

'A puppy,' Selby said. 'What a lovely gift. Okay, you can have a puppy.'

The girl's shocked mother waved her head from side to side.

'But Mummy said I can't have one,' the girl said.

'But dogs are wonderful,' Selby said. 'They are the best friend a little girl could have. They give you their love no matter what happens. And they're good for you too because they teach you to look after another living thing. They teach you responsibility.'

Selby looked at the girl's mother. The woman sighed and then nodded slowly.

'I think you've got your puppy, kid,' he whispered in the girl's ear.

'Oh, thanks Santa!' she said, giving Selby a big kiss.

For the next hour Selby had a wonderful time listening to kids' Christmas wishes.

'Hey, this is fun,' Selby thought. 'I like being Santa Claus. I think I'm good at it. And this Santa has *claws* at the end of his *paws*. Ho ho ho, that was a good one.'

Just at the end of Santa Time, two boys jumped on Selby's lap. And not just any two boys but the dreaded Willy and Billy!

'You boys behave yourselves,' Aunt Jetty said. 'Talk to Santa and I'll be back in a tick.'

'You look stupid, Mr Santa, stupid in a stupid suit,' Willy said after his mother had gone.

'Yeah,' said Billy. 'You're not the Santa.'

'Ho ho ho,' Selby laughed. 'What nice little boys you are. What do you want for Christmas?'

'I want a . . . I want a real tank with real guns that work, stupid-face,' Willy said. 'I'll bet you can't get me one.'

'Oh, yes I can,' Selby sang. 'I'll drive it over on Christmas morning and blow up your house. That would be really funny, wouldn't it, boys. Ho ho ho.'

'Hey! You're not supposed to say that to us, stupid make-believe Santa,' Billy said, grabbing Selby by the beard and pulling it down over the chin of Selby's dog suit. 'Look, Willy! He's a dog!'

'Time's up,' Selby said. 'Santa has to get back to the North Pole.'

'It's Selby!' Willy squealed. 'He's Selby in that suit — and he can talk!' 🐾

'Rack off, kid,' Selby whispered, 'before I thump you.'

'Mummy!' Willy screamed. 'Selby is playing Santa Claus! Hey, Mummy! Look! He's a dog in there! Hey, Billy, let's pull his head off!'

🐾 *Paw note: I wish I'd never talked to Willy, but I did — a few times.* S

Selby was running towards the storeroom when Willy and Billy tackled him around the legs.

'Get away from me, you monsters!' Selby whispered.

In a second, Billy was sitting on his chest tugging at the head of his dog suit. Selby grabbed it and struggled to keep it on.

'Get off me!' he yelled.

'I'm going to pull your head off and make you talk!' Willy screamed. 'You're a dog and you talk! I know you, you stupey poopey dog!'

Selby struggled to his feet.

'I'll take a short-cut through the Glassware Section,' he thought, 'to get to the storeroom door!'

Selby made a dash for the Glassware Section as a glass bowl whizzed by him, smashing into a glass case filled with plates. Selby turned just in time to duck as Billy threw a vase and his brother threw another one.

'Stop this right now!' the store manager screamed. 'Stop it, you hooligans!'

But now the boys were throwing everything they could get their hands on at the manager. The guard was now behind him, also ducking as glass smashed everywhere.

'He's a talking dog!' Willy screamed. 'That's no poopey Santa poopey Claus — that's Selby and he's a dog and he can talk!'

Selby slammed and locked the storeroom door behind him, threw off the rest of the Santa suit, and grabbed the gift-wrapped vase.

'Now to get out through the emergency exit!'

Selby could hear Aunt Jetty's booming voice: 'Willy! Billy! Stop that immediately!'

'It's not my fault!' Willy screamed. 'It was that stupey doggy, Mummy!'

'You're going to pay for every last broken item in this store, madam,' the manager said.

Selby picked up the gift and listened to the lovely sounds of Aunt Jetty's hand hitting the boys' bottoms and the wonderful sounds of their screams.

It was a beautiful, warm Christmas morning as Selby watched the Trifles unwrap their presents.

'This one's for you, Selby,' Mrs Trifle said, opening it. 'It's one of those yummy plastic bones that tastes just like the Dry-Mouth Dog Biscuits that you love so much.'

'Oh, well,' Selby thought. 'It's the thought that counts.'

'And what's this?' Dr Trifle wondered, grabbing the last present from under the Christmas tree. 'It says, "To Mrs Trifle, from Santa". Here, you'd better open it.'

'But who's it from?' Mrs Trifle asked, as she started to unwrap it. 'I know, it's from you, isn't it, dear? Oh, look! A vase just like the one that got broken! Thank you so much!'

'I'm sorry, but it's not from me,' Dr Trifle said, admiring it. 'It really isn't.'

'Then who could it be from?'

'The only person it could possibly be from,' Dr Trifle said, 'is Aunt Jetty. She must have finally found a vase like the one her boys broke.'

'Yes, of course!' Mrs Trifle said. 'Isn't she sweet. I take back everything I thought about her.'

'She's not a bad woman, your sister,' Dr Trifle said. 'She's really very thoughtful when she wants to bc.'

'Oh, no,' Selby thought. 'All that and who gets the credit? Aunt Jetty!' Selby looked at the warm smiles on the Trifles' faces. 'Oh, well,' he thought. 'I guess Mrs Trifle was right — *giving* is the most important thing.'

O Handsome Me

O handsome me, O handsome me
Who needs a fancy pedigree?
I see my face in mirrored glass
And say, 'Now *there* is doggy class.'

Now hang on! How can I be *hand* some
I've got no hands but only paws
A dog with hands would be quite awesome
I guess the word for me is *paw* some.

Selby Splits

'Mirrors are strange things,' Dr Trifle said. 'I've never really understood them.'

'What's to understand?' asked Mrs Trifle. 'You look and you see yourself in them.'

'That's what's so strange,' Dr Trifle said. 'You see yourself *in them*. You're *in* them but you're also *outside* them. It's as if there are two of you. Sort of the real you and then . . . well, some kind of a ghost.'

'A ghost! Sheeesh!' sheeeshed Selby. 'That gives me goosebumps.'

Dr Trifle poured another smelly chemical into his mixing bowl.

'So what are you inventing this time, dear?' Mrs Trifle asked.

'You asked me to clean the bathroom mirror before tonight's party so I've invented a special mirror cleaner,' Dr Trifle said, pouring the liquid into a spraying bottle and then scribbling on the label.

'What's wrong with the Quick 'n' Streaky Window Cleaner we buy at the shops?'

'That's made for windows — and other glass things too — but my new KleerSparkle Kleener is just for mirrors. Let's see if it works. I'll try it out on the mirror in the workroom.'

Mrs Trifle and Selby followed Dr Trifle into Dr Trifle's workroom. First Dr Trifle sprayed the big mirror with Quick 'n' Streaky. Then he sprayed it with his new formula. But when he did, something strange happened. First there was a high-pitched noise that stopped as quickly as it began.

'Ouch!' Selby thought. 'That hurt my ears! But the Trifles didn't seem to hear it. It must have been one of those sounds that only dogs can hear.'

As Selby watched, the surface of the mirror seemed to move in and out very slowly. Suddenly the mirror became as clear as an open window.

'Is that clean enough for you?' Dr Trifle asked with a grin.

'Goodness!' Mrs Trifle exclaimed. 'I feel like I could reach out and shake my own hand.'

'It's fantastic!' Selby thought. 'I already had goosebumps but now I've got goosebumps on my goosebumps! I can see every hair of my fur perfectly!'

'I will sell my formula,' Dr Trifle said, 'and we will become fabulously wealthy and then we'll give all the money to worthy causes.'

'Better wait a few days before you start giving away the money you don't have yet,' Mrs Trifle warned. 'Remember the disaster with your Breath-Away Miracle Window Cleaner?' 🐾

'How could I forget?' Dr Trifle said. 'It went all cloudy after a couple of hours and you couldn't see through the windows at all.'

'Exactly. So let's leave it for a day or two before we get too excited.'

When the Trifles left the house to do some last-minute shopping for the party, Selby dashed into the workroom. The mirror was as clear as before.

🐾 *Paw note: See the story 'Selby in Suspense' in the book* Selby Supersnoop. S

'Mirror, mirror on the wall,' Selby said out loud. 'Who's the handsomest dog of all? I am! I am! Oh, you beautiful poochypie.'

Selby often kissed himself in the mirror but this time he gave himself a big doggy lick. And as he did he heard a faint *plop* sound as tiny ripples spread across the surface of the mirror like the waves from a pebble dropping in a pond. Then Selby felt his tongue touching another tongue!

'Yuck!' he screamed, jumping back.

Selby could see his mouth move in his reflection but his reflection didn't jump back the way Selby had. His reflection just stood there with its paws on its hips.

'This is impossible!' Selby thought. 'He's not doing what I'm doing!'

Selby jumped up and down a couple of times while his reflection stood still. Finally, his reflection reached its paw out to the mirror.

Very slowly, Selby reached out towards his reflection. When his paw touched the mirror, once again there were ripples. Only this time, Selby's paw went through the surface of the mirror.

Selby's reflection grabbed his paw and jumped through to Selby's side of the mirror.

'Thanks,' it said. 'I thought I was stuck in there forever.'

'You talked!' cried Selby.

'Well? So did you. Hey, it's nice out here. Thanks, mate.'

Selby just stood there, numb, dumbfounded.

'I've split,' he said, looking in the mirror and not seeing either of them. 'There's two of me! I've multiplied! Or maybe I've been divided! Oh, no! Something terrible and mathematical has happened to me!'

'Don't be upset,' Selby's reflection said. 'You just saved me from the most boring job in the world.'

'But you can't stay here,' Selby said.

'Why not?'

'Because then I won't have a reflection.'

'What do you need a reflection for? Haven't you admired yourself enough? All that kissing and licking — you do it all the time.'

'That's not the point. If people see that I don't have a reflection then . . . then it'll be weird. They'll think I'm a vampire or something.'

'What's a vampire?'

'It's a bat person who sucks blood. They don't have reflections.'

'Sheeesh!' Selby's reflection said, looking around quickly. 'Are there any vampires here?'

'No, they're make-believe.'

'Then what are you worried about? I'm never going back there again.'

Selby's reflection grabbed the bottle of Quick 'n' Streaky from the floor and sprayed the mirror.

'What are you doing?' Selby yelled.

The reflection tapped the mirror with its paw.

'There, back to normal,' it said.

'But it's not back to normal,' Selby protested. 'I still don't have a reflection! Everyone has a reflection. It's a part of them. I don't. I've split.'

'You can't have everything, mate. And talking of splitting, I'm out of here.'

Selby raced after his reflection and found it in the kitchen opening the fridge.

'What are those people like?' it asked.

'What people?'

'The dude with the glasses and his wife, old curly locks.'

'They're my owners,' Selby said. 'They're the most wonderful people in the world.'

'Your *owners*? What are you, their slave or something?'

'No, I'm a dog, a pet dog. The Trifles love me and look after me.'

'Yeah, well that's great. I'll tell you what — nobody owns this dog.'

'You're not a dog,' Selby said. 'You're just the reflection of a dog — of me. You're the other part of me. The part that's *supposed to stay in the mirror*!'

'That was then and this is now,' Selby's reflection said, grabbing a platter from the fridge.

'Hey, put those back!' Selby said.

'Why? What are they?'

'They're peanut prawns — prawns cooked in peanut sauce from The Spicy Onion Restaurant. They're for the Council and Citizens' Party tonight.'

'Peanut prawns? Sounds terrible but we like them, do we?'

'I don't know about you but *I* do,' Selby said, grabbing the platter.

'Check this food,' his reflection said. 'Where do I start?'

Selby slammed the fridge door and stood in front of it.

'You listen to me!' he said. 'There are a few things you don't know about living outside mirrors! We can't eat my owners' food.'

'Okay, okay, take it slow, Joe. Lighten up. The problem is that I'm hungry — very hungry. Like I've never eaten — ever. You've been filling your face since you were a pup.'

'You can have some of my food,' Selby said. 'It's down there in that bowl on the floor.'

Selby's reflection bit into a Dry-Mouth Dog Biscuit and spat it out.

'I can't eat that stuff!' it said. 'It tastes like cardboard — not that I've ever eaten cardboard. Why can't I have what's in the fridge? Are these Fifles stingy or something? Boy, have they ever got you dancing to their tune.'

'*Trifles*,' Selby corrected his reflection. 'Now listen to me.'

'Aye, aye, admiral,' his reflection said, saluting.

'You're going back in the mirror right now.'

'No way.'

'Yes, you are.'

'Am not.'

'Are so.'

'Aren't.'

'Are.'

'Aren't.'

'Are.'

'Aren't.'

'Are.'

'Aren't.'

'Are.'

'Aren't.'

'Are.'

'Aren't.'

'Are.'

'Aren't.'

'Are.'

'Aren't.'

'Are.'

It suddenly dawned on Selby that his reflection was exactly as stubborn as he was and that this could go on all day.

'Okay, have it your way,' Selby said. 'But

there's one very important rule you have to learn.'

'Shoot.'

'We're not allowed to talk when anyone's around.'

'First you want me to be a slave and now you want me to be a *silent* slave?'

'The Trifles don't know that I — we — can talk. Nobody knows. Nobody except Willy but nobody believes a word Willy says.'

'They don't know you can talk? Why not?'

'Because it would shock them. Dogs can't talk.'

'What do you mean dogs can't talk. You're a dog and you can talk. I'm a dog and I can talk. Let's vote on it — okay, everyone who thinks that dogs can talk put up a paw.'

Selby's reflection put up its paw.

'You don't understand,' Selby said. 'I'm the only talking dog in Australia and, perhaps, the world.'

'Far out!'

'And remember that you're me. That's the only reason that you can talk.'

'I'm not you.'

'Yes, you are.'

'No, I'm not.'

'Are so,' Selby said. 'But I'm not going to argue. Point number one — if the Trifles knew I could talk they'd put me to work.'

'Would they?'

'Maybe not at first. But after a while they'd get used to me being a talking, reading and writing dog and then it would start. "Oh, Selby, would you mind making the beds while we're out? You don't have anything to do and we're really busy. That's a good dog." And that would just be the beginning. Do you want to work?'

'Me? Work?' Selby's reflection said. 'Are you kidding?!'

'Point two — if the word got around that there was a talking dog living here there would be people standing all around the house with cameras and binoculars trying to get a look at me. If I went to the loo in the bushes I'd have TV news camera crews filming me.'

'So you could stay inside.'

'And be trapped in the house for the rest of my life?'

'It's got to be better than being stuck in a mirror,' Selby's reflection said. 'Is there a point three?'

'Yes — dognappers.'

'Dognappers?'

'Dognappers. A talking dog would be worth squillions of dollars — maybe even grillions. I might be captured and held for ransom or sold to a very rich person to be kept in their private zoo.'

'Could that really happen?'

'It already did.'

'How'd you get away?'

'It's too complicated to tell you right now. You'll have to read the story "Selby Sold" in the book about me called *Selby Snaps!*'

'There's a book about you?'

'There are a few.'

'Who wrote them? Did you?'

'Sort of,' Selby said, seeing the Trifles arriving at the front door. 'The Trifles are coming! Quick! Back in the mirror!'

'*You* go,' his reflection said. 'I'm staying here.'

'Then at least hide!' Selby whispered.

'Where? I don't know where to hide in this house. All I know is the workroom. And the bathroom and the bedroom — only where there are mirrors.'

'Don't you dare say a word to anyone!' Selby whispered as he dived behind the lounge.

The Trifles came in carrying bags of groceries.

'Hello, Selby, old thing,' Mrs Trifle said as she patted Selby's reflection. 'My you look bright and happy today.'

'Yes, he does, doesn't he?' Dr Trifle said. 'He looks like a new dog.'

Selby watched from the crack between the lounge and a chair as his reflection wagged its tail and then sat down, putting his paw up for Dr Trifle to shake.

'Look at this!' Dr Trifle exclaimed. 'Selby's shaking hands! He hasn't done that since he was a puppy! Good boy!'

Now the reflection put two paws up.

'Goodness me,' Mrs Trifle said, 'he's begging. He's never done that. It's as though he has a split personality — one minute he won't do the simplest trick and the next minute he's sitting up and begging. Give him something to eat, dear.'

Dr Trifle picked up a Dry-Mouth Dog Biscuit and threw it. The reflection caught it perfectly in its mouth, held it for a moment and then placed it gently on the floor.

'I think he's gone off them,' Dr Trifle said. 'Give me a piece of that honey ham.'

'But that's for tonight.'

'Just a little piece. Come on.'

Mrs Trifle peeled off a slice of ham and threw it to the reflection, who caught it in its mouth and ate it.

'Look how happy that made him,' Dr Trifle said. 'Give him some of that double smoked island cheese.'

'It's very expensive,' Mrs Trifle said. 'Oh, well.'

This time the reflection caught the piece of cheese and, instead of eating it straightaway, it placed the cheese on the dining room table, and then hopped up onto a chair and ate it.

'I can't believe it!' Mrs Trifle exclaimed. 'He not only wants to eat people food, he wants to eat at the table like a person!'

'I can't believe it either,' Selby thought, smelling the wonderful smell of honey ham and double smoked cheese. 'Two minutes and he's got them trained!'

That afternoon Selby dodged from one hiding place to another as his reflection ate lots of the food Mrs Trifle was preparing for the big party. And when it wasn't eating, it was outside chasing sticks for Dr Trifle.

'It took me years to get Dr Trifle *not* to throw sticks for me and now it's all undone,' Selby thought.

Later he heard Dr Trifle say to Mrs Trifle, 'We're not going to be rich this time.'

'Didn't your mirror cleaner work?' Mrs Trifle asked, handing Selby's reflection a large piece of chocolate cake.

'I'm afraid the mirror's gone back to normal,' Dr Trifle said. 'Oh, well, I can't remember how I made it anyway. Easy come, easy go.'

That evening Selby lay in the darkness in the garage, listening to the music and laughter from the party. He thought of the wonderful life he'd led right up to the moment when Dr Trifle invented his KleerSparkle Kleener. It had been such a good life when there was only one of him.

Selby peeked out through a hole in the wall to see the backyard filled with people talking and laughing. Selby watched as his reflection began moving to the music. Everyone turned to watch as the reflection made its way around the yard in time to the music.

'Look! Your dog is actually moving to the beat!' one of the women said.

'He's a smart dog,' Mrs Trifle said, 'but he's changed recently. Suddenly he seems almost . . . human.'

'The next thing you know he'll be talking,' a man said with a laugh.

'Oh woe,' Selby thought. 'My reflection's going to give my — our — secret away for sure.'

Selby watched as his reflection made its way into the crowded house, being patted by everyone as it went. In a minute Selby heard a voice behind him.

'Oi! You in there?' it said. Selby's reflection stood in the doorway. 'It's me — your better half. What's wrong, mopey-bottom?'

'Don't you call me mopey-bottom, you traitor,' Selby said.

'Steady on, mate. Don't get your fur in a flap. What have *I* done?'

'You're going to give everything away.'

'I'm just having a good time,' Selby's reflection said. 'I guess I'm just a party animal. Are you jealous?'

'No, I'm not jealous.'

'Are so.'

'Am not.'

'What would you be doing if I wasn't here? Would you be out there where the action is?'

'Probably not.'

'Exactly. You'd be lying here in the garage hiding — which is what you're doing anyway. So don't be a spoilsport. Here, I brought you some food.'

Selby's reflection threw some Dry-Mouth Dog Biscuits on the floor.

'You could at least have brought some peanut prawns.'

'So now you want people food, is that it? I'll see if I can get some nibblies.'

'We've got to talk,' Selby said.

'Later. I'm having too much fun right now.'

'Well don't give our secret away.'

'I'll try not to.'

'Oh, and don't fall in the swimming pool.'

'Why not?'

'Because we can't swim.'

'Any other warnings, Mr Worrywart?'

'Look out for Aunt Jetty.'

'Aunt Jetty? Mrs Trifle's sister, Jetty? I just met her.'

'And?'

'She was a bit funny at first but a couple of

licks and now she thinks I'm fantastic. Gotta go, sport.'

'Great,' Selby thought. 'My reflection's even made friends with Aunt Jetty. That does it, now I'm going to have to kill him. But how will I do it? I know, when no one's looking, I'll push it in the swimming pool. But what if it calls for help? Then my secret will be out.'

Selby lay there thinking of guns and bombs and poisoned prawns.

'What am I thinking?! I *can't* kill my reflection. If I did then I wouldn't have a reflection any more. Everybody's gotta have a reflection. My only chance is to get it to go back in the mirror and stay there. But how? I can't make it. My reflection is just as strong as I am.'

Selby's mind started ticking over faster than it had ever ticked over before.

'I've got to outsmart it!' he thought. 'It's just as smart as I am, so what I need is *confidence*! I think I can. I think I can. I think I can.'

Suddenly in a distant desert, a stream of water spouted from the sand. Somewhere a cyclone stopped. In the depths of space a comet wobbled in its orbit and then sped on. And in this magic moment, the perfect plan settled into

Selby's brain — an idea so simple that it frightened him.

'I know I can! Yesssssss!' Selby whispered.

In the cool of the evening, most of the partygoers moved inside. Selby crept through the bushes. Nearby, Selby's reflection lay on a banana lounge catching the chocolates in its mouth that Aunt Jetty threw.

'I had no idea you were so much fun,' she squealed, as the reflection snapped another one out of the air. 'Ooops, finished the Swiss chockies. I'll see if I can find that box of Belgian ones.'

'Arooooooooo,' Selby's reflection barked.

Aunt Jetty giggled and went to the table on the other side of the yard.

'Hey! Psssst!' Selby said.

'What's that? A talking bush?'

'It's me, Selby, you idiot. Something serious has come up.'

'How serious?' his reflection asked.

'Deadly serious. Meet me in the workroom in ten minutes.'

'What if I don't want to?'

'Just be there.'

'Gotcha, chief.'

Selby was waiting in the workroom when his reflection arrived. He closed the door after it. The first thing the reflection noticed was that Selby had sprayed the mirror with KleerSparkle Kleener.

'Oh, no, you don't,' the reflection said. 'I'm not going in there again. No way, hoe-*zay*.'

'One of us has to go,' Selby said. 'It's either you or me. We can't have a reflectionless dog walking around.'

'Then it's you.'

'We'll flip a coin.'

'No way! I might lose.'

'Then how are we going to decide?'

'I've already decided,' the reflection said. 'You're going in. It's the perfect place for you. You don't have to do anything except take it easy all day and, occasionally, look at me. I promise not to kiss you.'

'Gee, thanks.'

Suddenly there were footsteps in the hallway.

'Someone's coming!' Selby whispered. 'Hide!'

'But there's no place to hide.'

'I'll help you into the mirror!' Selby said. 'We can't have them open the door and find both of us in here — and with no reflections! That would be a dead giveaway!'

'They're probably not even coming here,' the reflection said. 'They're probably heading down the hallway to the loo.'

'We can't take that chance!' Selby said. 'There's no lock on the workroom door. If they open it, we're gone! Come on, into the mirror! I'll let you out later.'

Selby's reflection smiled.

'Oh, no, you don't,' it said. 'You can't outsmart me that easily.'

'Okay then it'll have to be me,' Selby sighed. 'Help me in. Here, touch my paw, it only seems to work when we're touching.'

Selby's reflection touched Selby's paw and Selby stepped into the mirror. Just as he did, the reflection sprayed the mirror with Quick 'n' Streaky.

'Gotcha!' it said. 'Now *I'm* the dog and *you're* the reflection! So long, sucker! And guess what? whoever that was in the hallway just went into the loo — just as I thought.'

Selby looked around him in the mirror room. It was just like the workroom except the writing on the calendar was backwards.

'Please don't leave me in here,' he pleaded to his reflection. 'I don't want to spend the rest of my life — and that means *your* life — in a mirror.'

'Now you know how I feel.'

'But you're meant to be a reflection. That's your job. That's your purpose in life.'

'Purpose shmerpose,' the reflection said. 'In a few minutes you'll be just the way I was. You'll have to do everything I do. You won't be able to talk to me like this. The only thing you'll be able to do by yourself is think.'

'Please let me out,' Selby pleaded. 'I'll do anything you say.'

'Hmmm,' hmmmed the reflection as he looked at the Quick 'n' Streaky bottle. 'Why is the mirror still so clear? It should have gone back to normal. Oh, well, I'd better go and make my announcement.'

'What announcement?'

'I'm going to tell everyone at the party that I know how to talk.'

'You're going to tell — our secret?!'

'Why not? I don't know why you didn't do it years ago.'

'You know very well why I didn't!'

'Listen, I'm not like you, okay? I may look like you but I'm not like you. I'm not afraid of fame.'

'But you'll be kept in a laboratory and asked stupid questions by scientists all day.'

'If they ever did that I'd give 'em some dough and they'd let me go. Remember, I'm going to be very rich. There will be TV appearances, movies made about me, books written about me — not like the ones about you. These'll be *real* books about a *real* talking dog.'

'My books are about a real talking dog — me.'

'Yeah but nobody believes it because you won't tell them your real name or where you really live. I'm going to tell *everything*! Except the part about you being stuck in the mirror and me being your reflection, of course.'

'Somebody will dognap you.'

'I'll hire bodyguards. Why didn't *you* think of that, dummy?'

'The bodyguards might kidnap you.'

'I'll worry about that when the time comes,' the reflection said. 'See you when I see you.'

'Okay, you win,' Selby sniffed. 'Go ahead, tell the world. But there's one thing.'

'Is this another one of your lame-brained tricks?'

'You can't make your big announcement looking like that.'

'I look just like you!'

'Except for that piece of chocolate on your lip. It looks stupid. If you're going to give away the greatest secret in the history of the world you don't want to look like a slob when you do it.'

The reflection licked its lips.

'Did I get it?'

'Almost.'

Again the reflection licked.

'No good,' Selby said. 'This is where you need a real reflection to show you where it is. Here, put your mouth down close so I can show you.'

The reflection put its mouth close to the mirror and, just as it did, Selby reached out and pulled it through, jumping out at the same time.

'Hey! You tricked me!' the reflection screamed.

Selby grabbed the bottle of KleerSparkle Kleener (which was really Quick 'n' Streaky because Selby had switched the contents of both bottles) and sprayed the mirror, sealing his reflection behind the glass forever. In a minute, the reflection was doing just what Selby was doing — pouring the real KleerSparkle Kleener down the sink.

'Mirror mirror, on the wall,' Selby said with a grin. 'Who's the cleverest dog of all? Me!'

'Selby seems to be his old self again,' Mrs Trifle said as she cleaned up on the morning after the party. Selby lay on the floor nearby, watching and listening. 'I was a bit worried about him last night.'

'So was I,' Dr Trifle said.

'He did the oddest things,' Mrs Trifle said.

'All that stick chasing nearly wore me out,' Dr Trifle said.

'And he sat at the table and ate like a person. He even ate peanut prawns,' Mrs Trifle said. 'Imagine a dog liking peanut prawns!'

'Maybe he does like them,' Dr Trifle said.

'Heaven's no. No real dog would like peanut prawns. Here, watch this.'

Mrs Trifle put a pile of peanut prawns in Selby's bowl. She then put a Dry-Mouth Dog Biscuit on the floor beside it.

'Here, Selby,' she said.

The smell of peanut prawns suddenly filled Selby's nostrils. His mouth hovered over the bowl.

'I want them, I want them,' Selby chanted in his brain. 'But I can't have them!'

Selby's quivering mouth made its way down to the bowl but then quickly moved to the side and grabbed the dog biscuit.

'See?' Mrs Trifle said. 'Just as I thought — he's a normal dog. He's the dear old Selby that we love so much.'

'And that's what I'll always be,' Selby thought. And as he looked up at his wonderful owners, a little tear of happiness ran down his nose.

THROUGH THE LICKING-GLASS

Sometimes a mirror is called a 'looking-glass'. I should have called the last story 'Selby **through the licking-glass**'. If you've read the story, you'll know why. See what I mean about mirrors being spooky? Now I can never look in one without wondering if that's another me in there — a different me that only looks like me but isn't.

Sheeeeeeesh!

Anyway, thanks again for coming along on these adventures. It was great to have you with me. Now I feel all warm and fuzzy. Come to think of it, I am all warm and fuzzy — I'm a dog!

CYA

Selby

About the Author

Duncan Ball is an Australian author and scriptwriter, best known for his popular books for children. Among his most-loved works are the Selby books of stories plus the collections *Selby's Selection*, *Selby's Joke Book* and *Selby's Side-Splitting Joke Book*. Some of these books have also been published in New Zealand, Germany, Japan and the USA, and have won countless awards, most of which were voted by the children themselves.

Among Duncan's other books are the Emily Eyefinger series about the adventures of a girl who was born with an eye on the end of her finger, and the comedy novels *Piggott Place* and *Piggotts in Peril*, about the frustrations of twelve-year-old Bert Piggott forever struggling to get his family of ratbags and dreamers out of the trouble they are constantly getting themselves into.

Duncan lives in Sydney with his wife, Jill, and their cat, Jasper. Jasper often keeps Duncan company while he's writing and has been known to help by walking on the keyboard. Once, returning to his work, Duncan found the following word had mysteriously appeared on screen: ikantawq. . . . .

For more information about Duncan and his books, see Selby's web site at: **www.harpercollins.com.au/selby**